FROM
WHERE
WE
CAME

FROM WHERE WE CAME

BURT RASHBAUM

Story Sanctum
PUBLISHING

This is a work of fiction. Any likeness to real people or places is purely coincidental.

Cover image: Casselberry Creative Design via Wix AI Image Creator.

Cover design and interior formatting provided by Casselberry Creative Design.

Story Sanctum Publishing, LLC

ISBN: 979-8-9928559-2-0

For Sharon

In loving Memory, always

and

for Finnigan, our family's newest American

Table of Contents

Going Under

I'm not afraid. I know now I don't have much time but still, I am not afraid. When I chose to do this, or more truthfully, when I was chosen, I knew this was one outcome. At first I fought what happened, I used my strength to call out, to scream, but I knew that the ship would not turn around, and probably no one heard my cries for help anyway.

I know I won't be remembered. I have no wife, no children. My Mama and Papa think of me as dead. There will be no candle lit for me on the anniversary of my death, because no one will know I died. I will disappear into the blackness of this ocean when Death decides to take me, and I will go.

I made choices that it is too late to regret. I left my home in our little corner of Budapest because, had I stayed, there would be no future I could embrace. What would have happened? I would have been matched with some girl in our shtetl and would have married without love and had children I didn't want and been weighted with responsibilities – in fact a whole life – that I would have detested. I saw the ignorance from whence I came. How they all feared an invisible God that was like a fairy tale. I knew it was all lies.

Even my best friend Menasheh, he swallowed it all. My Papa insisted I go to yeshiva, and I would argue with Menasheh, I would mock him and the others, until finally I had to leave them behind. But Menasheh, he took the road I did not. I saw the stupidity of my people, and it was so easy to take advantage and never be found out. At first I would steal bread from the market. Then I grew bolder, and maybe it was a pair of new shoes from the cobbler, in and out of his shop before he could even look up and notice a pair was gone. But I understood this could not keep up. If I was caught, I would have to deal with the Goyim police. So I left one night without a goodbye to my Mama, without a note, gone like a puff of smoke from my Papa's fetid pipe.

And ran away to Hamburg. First I lived on the streets, sleeping in alleys and eating what I could swipe. On a day when my clothes were no more than tatters and I was skin and bones, freezing from rain, desperate for food, clumsy and dizzy from hunger, and when I reached for a loaf from a cart in an open market, a man I hadn't seen was faster than me. I felt him before I saw him, his hand grabbing my wrist as if I was enclosed in iron, and he said, "No." And without letting go, he dragged me down the street as I tried to pull free, but it was useless. I was weak. I thought he would bring me to the authorities, but instead we stopped at an open cart selling food and before I knew it he'd bought hot rolls stuffed with meat.

"I will let you go," he said, "but if you want this food, you will stand by me while we both eat."

I did as I was told. And that was when my life of crime began.

It was a long time between that first meal and my going to America on that ship. My benefactor became my teacher and then my friend.

They told me I would be bringing a treasure stolen from the Tsar across the ocean, and when I arrived, I would be rewarded. But I knew how to read the newspaper. I believed the Tsar wouldn't last, that the treasure would never be used to keep him in power from half a world away. I knew the criminals who arranged for this to happen. They planned the whole thing so they would be rich, and I would be paid handsomely and begin a new life. But I had my own plan. When the ship arrived in New York, I would escape with the riches in my crate and I would make a life for myself far from the old world.

But I never expected to see Menasheh on that ship. How did he come to leave his safe and comfortable life in Budapest? I knew he saw me, but it was only after I had been discovered. I never thought there would be spies on the ship keeping an eye on me, spies from a rival group who had their own plans for what was hidden in my crate.

They never saw which crate was mine, when I was finally discovered. They tried to beat the truth out of me, and when I wouldn't talk, they chased me. And then caught me. And tried again to beat me, but I fought them with all my strength.

But they were too much, and they threw me over.

And here I am, weakening, the ship now a speck in the distance. I am done with the fighting. I have no more strength. I am tired. I am cold. I am sleepy. So I will close my eyes.

Recorded Voices and a Sepia-toned Portrait

He only had one recording of his parents' voices. He had a lot of old home movies; his grandfather had a camera as far back as the 1940s, and there were many scenes over many years of his parents laughing, talking to the camera, holding him and his siblings as babies and then as they grew older. There were even ancient scenes from his aunt's 1947 wedding. So many clips of so many relatives – including his parents – now dead. But no voices. Only silent films, even those in color.

The one sound recording was made by his brother Jake, still living in his parents' house, still a teenager, back in the 70s. He had the idea, after Blake moved west to begin his life, to make a 'sound letter,' saying aloud what he'd usually write, and the plan was for he and his brother to trade tapes in the mail instead of words, and talk to each other.

The first – and only – time his brother did this, he

decided first to let his parents say a few words. His mother spoke quite naturally, as if she was talking to him in person. She talked of the house, the weather. Not much, but a few quick sentences. Then his father, given the mic, seemed awkward, listening now. His father pretended he was on the phone with him, long distance and expensive, so when he said, "Hey boy, how's it going?" his father waited as if there was a response on some imagined phone, and he could hear Jake cracking up. His father said, "Just watched Denver beat the Jets," then nothing more. Jake took the mic and continued on with that first, and only, taped letter.

Now, being older than both his parents when they died, when he listens to the recording, which he does on their yahrzheit days while the 24-hour candle burns down in memoriam, it feels like what he hears doesn't sound like them. Maybe because he's older than they ever were? He's not sure. Maybe because the only sounds of them he has are these few short uncomfortable sentences? Or maybe he's actually forgotten what they sounded like.

He thinks about his own son, and what he might have of his after he's gone. There's a lot of video, taken from his son's birth to his young adulthood, when he and Molly finally stopped recording every holiday or new event in their son's life. So his son would have a lot of movies of himself, and he'd hear his father talking behind the camera. Blake was never on camera, he was always filming. His son would have no visual, just sound, like he has with his own parents. Would his son eventually think, *what did he really look like? I have no visuals of him, moving, laughing, throwing me in the air. I only have his voice. Do I really remember what he looked like, even though I have lots of photos?*

When he listens to his parents' voices, he never plays the recording once. He'll immediately play it again. And again. Until he's convinced the speed must be wrong. The more he plays it, the less he's convinced they ever sounded like this. His mother never had such a thick Brooklyn accent. His father never sounded so tentative, so unsure.

Part of it, he knew, was that they were getting further away from him, receding deeper into the past. He felt like he knew what his grandparents sounded like better than what his parents sounded like – but that might be because he had no recordings of his grandparents, so their voices only existed in his memory.

Somehow the recording seemed less reliable than photographs, although in truth the recording was more reliable, maybe in the same way that a photograph was more reliable than a sample of handwriting. Look at someone's signature; do you know them at all? Maybe a bit. But then look at a photo of the person who signed their name – they come alive in a way more three-dimensionally than just some faded ink on paper. Then why didn't this work with a recording?

He was getting tangled up in this fun-house of memories, he knew, because of the old photo he'd recently found (again) that had been buried in an album he'd compiled of family photos he'd inherited from his mother after her death. She'd also had albums from her mother – his grandmother – and he'd taken all those, plus the ones he had, and put them in a huge book that was a five-generation compilation of his family. He probably had dozens of pics of his own nuclear family alone. He'd tried to put them in order, from faded sepia tones to early black and whites, to washed-out color of sixties Kodachrome, to prints from digital cameras. Going through the many pages of this huge tome was a visual narrative of his family, from the first portraits taken in a New World, to the latest shots showing modern America on the verge of the 21st century.

A lot of the people in the most ancient photos he didn't know. Maybe great-great-aunts or uncles? The backs of these pictures were blank: no names, no descriptions. Except one. He knew this one because it was unlike all the others.

A young man stands in front of a canvas army tent, looking proud, smiling at the photographer. He has an expression that seems to say, I know something you don't. He's in a fresh-pressed uniform of the World War I army, ready to take on the world, or at least the Germans.

This was his great-uncle Julius, his maternal grandmother's older brother. It's the only picture he has of this man, and on the back, in his grandmother's hand, is written, "My brother Julius," as if she herself might forget him.

This great-uncle died in the 1918 flu epidemic, and was never spoken of.

When he was very young, visiting his grandparents, he first saw the little candle burning in the small glass, the only light in the den no one ever sat in. He'd grasped the table, looking up at the flickering light, wondering why it was there, what it meant. He finally learned part of the answer when his mother found him there one time and came up behind him, putting her hands on his shoulders.

"That's for Uncle Julius," she said.

"Who's Uncle Julius?"

"Nana's brother. We light these candles for people in our family who died."

He had a lot more questions, but his mother led him out of the room. Question time was over.

His grandmother had a brother, other than his Great Uncle Sam? It was always Jennie and Sam, grandmother and great uncle, the only great uncle. It was much later that he understood a bit more about how important this missing uncle was in the family. His aunt's middle name was Julie. There were distant cousins of his parent's generation obviously named for him, cousins he'd see at Passover seders, Thanksgivings, various family events. Jill, Jack, Geraldine, Jonah, Jared, Jerry. A whole generation carried his name in some form. And yet, there were no photos of him but the one, he was never mentioned, and a candle was lit once a year that burned for 24 hours.

He never got to ask his grandmother about her brother, he never asked his mother about her missing uncle, and he never really needed to find out more about this uncle until he started listening to his parents' voices on that recording, when he realized, hearing them speak, that they didn't sound like his parents at all.

He'd stare, mystified, at that sepia-toned picture of a young man in uniform, smiling at the entrance of a canvas tent, knowing something he didn't.

Becoming Julius

He remembered rain, and Budapest as a dim gray shape beyond his view, the rooftops in the distance hidden by a dense wet fog. His leather suitcase on the bed, open and full to bursting, its brown straps frayed and brittle. His brother's on the floor, the straps tightly closed. Rain splattered the windows. The day was a miserable, cold spring; not a good one for traveling. His parents were preparing one last meal in this house, and then they'd say goodbye to the only world he'd ever known.

He held his tallis, its cotton smooth, with knotted corners that had barely been handled in the reverie of prayer, a gift from his grandfather, who also gave one to his brother Shmuel. Should he leave it behind? He stared at his brother's suitcase, not knowing if his was in there.

He folded the tallis gently, placing it atop his other belongings. Testing the suitcase, to see if it could close, he had fearful visions of it flying open somewhere on their journey.

His T'fillin, the phylacteries, were already at the bottom of his suitcase. He took no chances with this religious article. He'd said his morning prayers early, before the rain, draped in his tallis with his T'fillin wrapping his arm and his forehead, so he would be sure to have time to pack them carefully. He didn't even know if he believed in the rite, but he did it anyway. Maybe, in America, he'd feel differently.

Just then his mother walked into his room. She stood next to him in silence, only coming up to his shoulders.

"Moshe," she said, "finish after we eat."

His mother had been cooking all day. The house smelled of brisket with carrots and onions and challah baking. He pulled the leather straps around the suitcase, tightening them. His father entered his room. He and his father had never been close. His father worked hard to provide for the family, showed little affection, and prayed at the synagogue, although only on the highest holy days.

He put his suitcase on the floor; done at last.

"Frimmke," his father said to his mother, "come downstairs."

She gave his hand a squeeze and followed his father out.

His parents never learned English. He had been trying to learn the language for years because he wanted to read Mr. Mark Twain in the original. His younger brother and sister barely understood that they were going to the New World, but he knew of the adventure awaiting them. Mostly he felt fear about the journey, first a train to somewhere he'd never been, and then a huge boat where they would crowd into steerage.

The train ride from Budapest began with an aura of excitement. Their first destination was Hamburg and the Passagierin Halls. He was amazed to find thousands of expectant immigrants, all waiting for their ship to board. There were families, old men and women, the sick and the healthy. Their commotion made a thunderous din and he could hear the screams of children, crying, shouting, shrieking. His father held the tickets, and they needed to wait for the next day when their ship would be announced for departure. They spent the night in a filthy flophouse near the docks. His mother had hard biscuits for them to eat.

The ship was almost too massive for his eyes, with smokestacks billowing black clouds. They walked among hundreds of others, were led onto the ship, then down into steerage. He gripped his suitcase so tightly his knuckles were white. He, his brother, and sister held hands, his siblings holding their small suitcases tightly, and his mother and father surrounding them. He noticed the stares of the first-class passengers looking down from their own deck far above as they descended below, following a minor officer into dark halls, then were assigned iron bunks that contained only mattresses made of straw, many already coming apart, leaking brown strands.

He saw families clinging to one another, staying together for protection, like theirs, and groups of men eying all the steerage passengers, gauging from whom they could steal whatever they could get their hands on. His father said to them before they boarded the train, keep your suitcases within sight at all times! The floors were wood, and worn, scratched and rutted, but were swept every morning, then sprinkled with sand. Some mornings the new sand smelled worse than the day before, a choking damp.

There were lines, always lines, queuing up to eat, to shit, to wash. There were only two washrooms for steerage, both used by men and women at the same time. They had to wait with hundreds of others to do their daily business. The voyage was to last twelve days, and the few receptacles allowed to the steerage class for laundry or bathing soon became harder and harder to locate. There was nothing for those who became seasick, and by the third day the steerage area was unbearable, with a pale scent of vomit clouding his senses. His sister continuously wept. His brother only stared at the floor. His mother and father never spoke a word.

Some days he stayed in his bunk for most of the day. At night the gangs went to work. He heard women being attacked, crying and begging for mercy in foreign tongues. Small bands of men pounced on innocent sleeping passengers; he heard clubs pounding on flesh, the crack of bones, then trunks being dragged to another part of the hallway for looting. He fought sleep as much as he could, but always dozed off. He was shocked awake in the morning when children began running about. There was horror one morning as a mother discovered a dead child by her side, the sweeping panic as the cry "Typhoid!" ripped through the darkness. An infestation of lice was unavoidable, a horrible crawling itching everywhere, and by the fourth day there was blood under his fingernails, the taste of blood on his tongue. The smell of blood seemed to be a constant in the air, mixing with the other nauseating stenches, now thick.

Every day his mother handed out her biscuits, which were as hard as wood. She told them to suck on them until they softened.

His father brought them to the decks one at a time, while his mother guarded their luggage. From the decks he saw an ocean uninviting, mysterious and cold. But in steerage there seemed to be an ocean of hands: anonymous hands reaching for his body in the night as he let down his guard in exhaustion, women's hands reaching for tenderness or protection, men's hands reaching for a quick feel or trying to pick his pocket, children's hands reaching for anything. And there were the eyes, staring through him, burning, accusing, demanding, or waiting for him or his family to leave their bags unattended. He saw no friendly faces and spoke not a word the whole time. After a while he didn't even hear his own voice inside his head.

His sleepless nights and wasted days merged. He could not tell one from the other.

He recognized German, Italian, Spanish, Yiddish, but other languages remained a Babel to him. He witnessed arguments, fights that no one attempted to stop, saw one man stabbed in broad daylight. The man lay bleeding, his attacker vanishing in the surrounding crowd, until the ship's crew dragged him away.

The continuous rocking of the ocean churned his stomach. On days with his father on deck the sun was searing, but on the seventh and eighth days it stormed, and the heavens' blackness lasted beyond the borders of the night. The ship was flung on the water, hit with terrible waves, and there was now a slick veneer of vomit covering every bit of steerage floor space. In the endless dark his mother and sister wept without end. He tied his handkerchief around his face but it didn't help. He tried to walk to the bathroom once to be sick himself, but slipped on the wet sand that was soaked with vomit and fell in a pool of stinking phlegm. He retreated to his bunk, where he clung to his parents, along with his siblings, until the storms passed. The next day the passengers weren't allowed on the open decks; they had to spend the hot day in the horrible stinking darkness, as if they were being punished. He later found out that they had been banished from the clean air and dry calm seas so the first-class passengers could have free reign of the ship, to air out their own cabins.

The next night his father decided to get some air when darkness fell, and grabbed him by the wrist to accompany him. They stepped over people lying in the hallways, either unconscious or asleep. When they made it to the deck, he smelled sweetness, cleanliness, as he took a deep breath. The stars were brilliant. He relaxed as he exhaled. He had never seen such stars, never knew the sky could hold such a heaven as this. There were small groups of people standing around, and he heard the whispered conversation of a dozen different languages. From the other end of the ship he recognized the anger of the thugs who had taken to looting and bullying whoever they could. Suddenly a man came running their way. He saw terror in the man's eyes, and in an instant three others caught the man and began beating him, kicking him until his cries were barely audible. Then they lifted him without a moment's hesitation and threw him overboard. They looked in every direction, challenging anyone to accuse them. One pulled out a bottle and all of them drank. He glanced into the ocean, searching for any movement on the water, but there was nothing. His father grabbed his hand and they returned to their bunks, staying there until the middle of the next day, to the whimpering choking crying spasms of his brother and sister.

As the days passed he noticed a few families, like his, who huddled together in the dark corners of steerage, keeping to themselves. Men his father's age, protecting their families; girls his sisters' age, packed close to their mother, never venturing away by themselves. Finally, one day, there came a cry from the deck, then a cheer, then thunderous pandemonium. His father led them all up to the decks, making sure they had their small bags, and through the distant fog and mist of the ocean he saw it too. Land in the distance. The cry went out, in English, "Inspection! Inspection!" and he realized that this was the moment of truth: they would be taken in or be sent back. He explained this to his parents, and the look on his mother's face reflected his own panic. Everywhere there weren't people there was baggage: suitcases, bundles, sharp objects wrapped in rags, wooden containers, wicker baskets, boxes, trunks. His father pulled him away from his family, and sat him down firmly on a large crate that had two leather handles nailed into the sides.

"You tell them this is ours," he said, "and if they ask you what is inside, you say, gifts from your grandmother. You understand?"

He didn't understand. This wasn't their crate, but

no one else claimed it. He nodded. Then his father leaned close to him and whispered, "I know what this is. I knew the man they threw into the ocean. This is ours now. Can you do this?"

The ship passed through the narrows: there was land on either side. He couldn't believe the buildings in the distance. And the ships! There were so many other ships crowded into this one lane of water.

He tried to get a better view, as his father sat his siblings on the crate and told them not to move. He could tell his sister was relieved to not be standing in such a crowd. His brother looked terrified, too scared to cry.

There was a commotion over the side of the ship. A smaller boat appeared, and uniformed officers climbed aboard, one obviously a doctor. He could hear the crisp English being spoken, and he tried to remember the lessons he had stolen in moments of quiet, any words from Mark Twain. The doctor went from one to another, looking at them, occasionally pointing to a passenger.

Then a hushed silence came over the deck. He looked out to where everyone's gaze was drawn, and there she was, the great statue rising from the waters near the shore. She was beautiful. There was laughter and shouting, people were hugging and kissing each other. It was as if all the terrors of the previous days were imagined.

Off to the left of the statue he saw the red brick buildings of Ellis Island, and straight ahead the skyline of New York. Budapest seemed tiny by comparison. Even Hamburg was nothing compared to this.

When he heard his family name called, he practically

screamed in answer. His voice sounded alien to him; he barely recognized it. He and his father lifted the crate, and both his hands were now full, one gripping his battered suitcase, the other holding a leather strap nailed to the heavy crate his father also held. He had no idea what they were lugging. When they boarded the ferry they were each given a card with a letter and a number. The ferry docked at Ellis Island, and the crowds began leaving, dragging their whole lives with them.

He was able to read signs, hear English words, in this chaos. He followed the crowds, and led his family into a vast building. There were more lines, thousands of people, enough to fill a hundred ships. He understood that both men and women were able to shower, so he explained that his mother and sister should go one way, and he and his father and brother would watch their bags, and when they were finished they would switch. Afterwards he felt vaguely clean for the first time since their departure. But he hated showering in the presence of other naked men. He was quick, then out.

Their baggage was examined, including the mysterious crate, where he got a glimpse of its insides. He only saw rags wrapped around many items. He did as his father instructed, explaining these were from his grandmother back home. Then they stood in another line. They were of a group of 30 immigrants, as seven other groups of 30 were also moved to the large arena of the Registry Hall. There was noise everywhere, children screaming, thunderous horns of the ships outside. Inspection officers went from one passenger to another, looking at the card they were given. The officers wrote on a piece of paper and tagged the immigrants' clothing. He watched as an American came to him, taking the paper. The man looked at the number and letter, wrote it on some paper, and stuck the paper to his coat. Then he did the same with his parents, and his siblings. Then the whole group moved to lines according to the letter on their tags.

Groups of two and three men in white went from person to person, pieces of chalk in their hands. Some people were marked with an "H" or an "L" or an "X." This was clearly a health inspection, because many who received the "X" were obviously quite ill. A few who coughed wore the "L." His mother looked as if she would fall over with fear.

Then the doctors surrounded him, touching him, probing with their fingers. One doctor grabbed his head and stared into his eyes. Another pulled his ears, opened his mouth and looked inside as if he were a horse. A third pointed to a door, and spoke to him in quick English. He barely understood, but knew he was to go through the door. They hadn't marked him with any letter. He tried to explain that he had to wait for the others, but the man yelled at him to "Go! Go!" and he left his family, hoping they would soon join him. He knew this meant he was healthy enough to pass through. When he entered the door, there were lines leading up to small desks. He took his place at the back of one and slowly made his way to the front.

As he was about to get to the desk, he turned to see his family enter the room. He waved them over and they joined him, his father dragging the crate.

The man sitting before him began firing questions at such a speed he could hardly understand. The first was, "Your name?"

He didn't want to say his name. Standing here, in America, it suddenly sounded alien. He thought quickly, remembering the play he'd read, in English, trying to learn more than he could from Mark Twain.

"Julius," he said.

"Last name!" the man said.

Their surname was not a collection of sounds impossible to say in English, but he spoke slowly and watched as the man wrote down his new name, Julius, and his last name, which mostly remained the same.

"This is my family," he said, "can I help them answer for you?"

"Okay," the man said, looking at the paper before him, and began reading, "How did you pay for your passage? Do any of you have a job waiting? Are you joining relatives? Do you have an address? Where were you born? Where did you last reside? Are any of you anarchists?"

He answered as fast as he could, his whole body shaking as the man shouted the questions at him. They were headed to a place called Brooklyn where his father had a cousin. He felt like the fate of his family was in his hands, in his ability to speak this new language. He gave his siblings new names as well. Gdanke became Jenny, his brother Shmuel became Sam, both names from another English book he'd read. His father went from Menasheh to Max, and his mother became Dorothy, leaving Frimmke behind. He wasn't sure they were aware they now had

American names.

The last question made him stop. He was shaking from nerves, hunger, fear. His father stared at him with a look that was part terror, part anger.

"Anarchist?" he asked timidly.

"Yes, yes. Do you understand? Are any of you anarchists?"

"No, no anarchist."

"Okay then, here you go." The man gave him a card that was clearly stamped "ADMITTED," then handed one to each of his family, pointed to another door and shouted "Out!"

Ferry boats were leaving for the city. He hoisted his half of the crate by its leather handle, grabbed his suitcase, and led his family to the ticket gate, where they presented their cards to the man waiting, then he paid American money to board the ferry. He had enough left over for the required head tax. The steerage passengers had been allowed to change their currency on the ship, and when his father gave him all the German marks he had, that's when he knew he was now in charge of his family. Then they were once more on the water, heading to New York. For the first time he noticed how magnificent a day it was. The sky was as blue as the beautiful Danube of his Budapest. The air smelled sweet.

The ferry docked with a crash. And suddenly they were in the turmoil of a city he could never have imagined. The buildings, the crowds, more people than he had ever seen, the honking of so many automobiles, horses crowding the streets, young boys hawking newspapers, screaming in an English he barely understood. A noise that left him dizzy. So much life. It was paralyzing, electrifying, terrifying. For the first time, he allowed himself to say the word out loud.

"America."

And a stranger passing by looked at him, looked at them all, shook his head and laughed, and said, "That's right, America."

Menasheh

Although his name was Menasheh, which meant forgetful in Hebrew, he knew he was nothing of the sort. Remembering everything he'd ever seen, or read, made him the star of the Yeshivah in Budapest. His mother realized this trait of her son when he was young, so she'd take him to the market, and she'd say, how much was the chicken last time? And if it was less, she'd begin her bargaining before the chicken-monger could even say hello. If it was more the last time, he was to keep his mouth shut.

So he knew, or seemed to know, at least by sight, everyone in his shtetl-like neighborhood, where only Jews walked, talked, shopped, prayed, ate, stole, were born, died, and left never to return.

And he knew where those who left went: America. It was the only option for anyone in his world to break free of generations of tradition. It was the only place there existed any kind of hope, or opportunity, or a life not shackled to centuries of history, religion, and superstition.

His world began expanding beyond his family and their little house when he was old enough to finally be admitted to the religious school, the Yeshivah, where he would learn to read the prayers that guided his father's world, where he would be instructed in the Holy Torah, and where his parents hoped he would join the family tapestry, eventually marry, and carry on his family name.

This happened, but not in the way his parents hoped. He'd learned what was required of him, which was almost too easy, as once he read something, it stayed in his head from that second on. When questions were asked in his classes, his hand always went up. And if no hand went up, the rabbi would look at him and say, with a smile, "Menasheh, surely you remember what all the others have forgotten," making a joke because of the meaning of his name. And he always had the answers.

He became friends with a few boys who seemed completely disinterested in their learning. But they were fun to be with, and fun was something not allowed in the hallowed halls of learning and prayer. Still, they were the ones who he was attracted to; the only real excitement in his life was in the off-the-cuff conversations he experienced with these boys. They knew they would end up being on the low rungs of their world. But Menasheh somehow understood that, in time, he would move beyond them, and he thought that they all knew it as well; but for now, they accepted him.

His best friend was Yakov, who belonged in a Yeshivah as much as he belonged in a church. Yakov's parents enrolled him in classes to keep him in one place, out of trouble. It mostly worked. Menasheh liked the daring nonchalance that his friend adopted as his personal milieu. Sometimes it seemed like Yakov would say something outrageous, to the laughter of their cohorts, simply to see Menasheh's reaction.

Yakov was the first of his peers he'd ever seen with a cigarette. His own father didn't smoke, although his grandfather smoked an old pipe that stunk to the heavens. But the first time Menasheh saw Yakov pull out a pouch of tobacco and papers and roll himself a cigarette, in the rabbi's study no less, while they were on a break from their learning, he almost choked. The other boys looked on as well, wide-eyed, not believing this sacrilege.

"I'm going to America, as soon I can steal the money," Yakov said, licking the paper, sealing in the tobacco.

"Yakov, please, what are you doing?" Menasheh said.

An old Talmud, one long in disuse, was unrolled on the rabbi's table. They were supposed to be studying a passage on Exodus, but Menasheh knew their break-time was really a way for their rabbi to take some time to himself.

"You think you can get yourself across an ocean?" another of the boys said.

"It's the only way for me to break free of," Yakov waved his hand around the room, "this." He took a match from the pouch and struck it on the table, inches from the sacred parchment.

"Yakov, please, what are you doing!" Menasheh

said again.

The tiny stick burst into flame, and Yakov brought it to the tip of the rolled paper extended from his lips.

"Listen," he said, exhaling a cloud, "I know I'll be safe in America. I'll be my own man. I'll be out of reach of my parents, and you know what I will have?" They all looked at him. "I will have my freedom. America is freedom."

He pointed at the Talmud on the table, its ancient brittle paper, his hand holding the cigarette. The other boys, Menasheh included, held their breath as one.

"These words? We all know these words now, yes? And no one more than our friend Menasheh. These words will not help any of us, yes? What help will we get? There is no strength in these words. There is no power. This paper, with faded ink, this Talmud, what is it? Commentary from men who are long dead and buried."

Yakov inhaled deeply and the plume of smoke he blew to the ceiling formed a light cloud, floating above their heads.

Yakov flicked the ash off his cigarette, and one tiny spark flew onto the page. The ancient paper smoldered. None of them could believe it and they watched as the sacred text began to burn. Menasheh finally got up and slammed his hand down on the text.

"See?" Yakov said, visibly shaken, throwing the end of his cigarette out the window, "it's only paper. This paper burns as easily as the rags of the newspapers our fathers read with such interest."

After that day, Menasheh thought his friend was

not only reckless, but possibly dangerous. He didn't know then that this would be the last year his friend would attend Yeshivah. When the next year began, what would be Menasheh's last, his friend didn't show. He didn't see him anywhere in the neighborhood, and Menasheh wondered if he'd finally made the great leap, and somehow gotten the funds to get him across an ocean.

It was halfway through that last year when Menasheh began thinking about his future. One night his mother told him to remain seated after the meal had been cleared.

His father quickly went to the living room and buried his head in the newspaper. His mother cleared a few dishes, but did not begin washing. Then she sat down next to him and took his hand.

She looked at him with such a fierceness he had to finally look away. But she pulled his eyes back by tightening her grip.

"Menasheh," she said, "my son. You are the light of my life. Do you know this?"

"Yes, Mama," he said, thinking, *what did I do? How much trouble am I in?*

"And you know that when you were bar-mitzvahed you became a man."

"Yes, Mama. Everyone knows that is what that day means."

She dropped his hand and put her palms on the table.

"Today I met with Gitte."

He swallowed. Gitte was the matchmaker. Whatever he might have been expecting, he wasn't expecting this.

"Gitte?" he said, not quite so innocently.

"She said I came at the exact right time. She has known you all her life. She said she has been looking out for you in a way you could never have known."

No, he thought. I'm too young. Yakov would never stand for this.

His mother looked at him and raised her eyebrows.

"Nothing?" she said. "You don't want to know who?"

"Does it matter what I want to know?"

She laughed, leaned over, grabbed his face, and kissed his forehead.

"No, it does not matter. But she has also been looking out for another in the same way. Her match for you was in the making long before you became a man."

And with that, she stood up and went to the sink, began scraping food off the plates. Menasheh sat there, in a mild state of shock. Was that it? His mother knew who his wife would be, the matchmaker knew as well, but he was not supposed to know?

He went and stood next to his mother while she cleaned the dinner away. She smiled in a way that meant, yes, you are allowed to ask, though she didn't meet his eye.

"Mama," he said.

"She is from a very good family. You may have even seen her at the synagogue Chanukah parties when you were little."

"Mama."

She took a towel and wiped her hands. Then, turning to face him, with tears in her eyes, she said the name that would change his life.

"Frimmke," she said, and leaned up, and this time kissed him on the lips.

He glanced over at his father, sitting by the fire, pretending to read the newspaper. For a quick second he glanced up, over the headline, and looked into the kitchen. He caught Menasheh's eye, and Menasheh thought he could read his father's face, before he hid once again behind words of the world. Thank G-d that is over, he seemed to say, in that one glance, thank G-d it wasn't me who had to tell you.

He knew the time would eventually come. Gitte arranged almost all the marriages in his neighborhood, all the families who belonged to their synagogue. But he didn't expect it this soon. He didn't know what he expected. To have some time for himself? To carouse with Yakov, wherever he'd taken off to? He'd never given himself any time to really puzzle that out. But he knew it had to be. He would never go against the tradition. He would marry, he and Frimmke would have children, and he would settle himself into the community.

All of which happened. It turned out he knew Frimmke from more than an occasional synagogue party. When his mother took him to the market, to be the memory of past prices so her bargaining had more power, he would see Frimmke with her mother, also shopping. Her father had a greengrocer stall in the market, so she always seemed to belong there. They'd look at each other, and once Frimmke stuck her tongue out at him. Another time she put her thumbs in her ears and wiggled her fingers at him. He always liked this attention from this girl he didn't know. But he never knew this would be the girl he would marry.

The two families had a celebration dinner before the wedding. But Frimmke wasn't there. He expected to see her, hoped he'd be able to have a quick word with her, to say what, he had no idea, but only her parents walked in, with their younger daughter, her father carrying a basket of fresh vegetables, her mother carrying a challah. He watched them come in, he witnessed the stiff ceremony of politeness as the gifts were delivered to the kitchen, and he waited for another to walk in.

He went to the door, opened it, looked up and down the street.

"Menasheh," his mother said, "come inside. Where are you going?"

He understood. They wouldn't see each other until their wedding day. And he wouldn't see her face until he lifted her veil, after the rabbi pronounced them man and wife.

Menasheh seemed to float through his days until his wedding. For the first time, it seemed as if nothing he saw or heard stayed in his head. The only thing he heard that stuck was that, once he was married, he and Frimmke would live with her parents until they had their first child, and Menasheh would come to work with her father in the market to learn the produce trade so that when her father became too old, he could take over the stall.

Is that what I am to be, he thought, *a greengrocer? Is that to be my life?*

When the day came, he felt as if he was in a dream, calmer than he'd ever been, while a tumult of activity happened all around him. His mother had been cooking for days, Frimmke's mother was there every day, and all his friends – except Yakov – would say to him, the first to marry! His father helped him with his itchy wool suit that barely fit him, and when they walked to the synagogue, his father walked beside him with pride.

The only moment he could think of, that he looked forward to more than he would admit, was when he would reach over, lift Frimmke's veil, and see her face for the first time as his wife. The rest was all noise and confusion.

As they stood under the chuppah, the wedding tent held aloft by his father, Frimmke's father, and two of his dearest friends, and as the rabbi intoned the wedding prayers, for the first time he felt a nervous knot in his stomach. This was really happening. It was no dream. Here she was.

Then there was a huge silence, as if all those in the synagogue benches were suddenly frozen. The rabbi caught his eye, and motioned with his face, *now, now*!

He reached over, delicately took the veil in his hands, slowly lifted the lace. When their eyes met, everything else seemed to slip away. Here was Frimmke, waiting for him to kiss her. She closed her eyes and raised her face.

He'd never kissed a woman. Well, his mother, of course, but that was kissing his mother! He stared closely at her face, eyes closed, waiting. He thought her expression changed in a subtle way. As if she went from one of happiness to possibly fear, some kind of questioning happening behind her eyelids, and with every second they stood before each other, he saw a sadness he didn't want to ever see again.

He leaned over and put his lips on hers, keeping

them there longer than he knew was correct. When they parted and she opened her eyes, all the sadness was gone. She smiled at him in such a way that he thought, here is a sunshine my life has never had before.

"My wife," he said.

"My husband," she answered.

Their wedding night, even in all its expected awkwardness, was a night of kindness, patience, and wonder, for both of them. And although Menasheh felt like a stranger in his new wife's parents' home for a few weeks, there came a day when he felt like he was where he was supposed to be; even learning the greengrocer trade from his father-in-law was a task he accepted without question.

Then came Moshe, his first-born. Soon after, Shmuel, and then Gdanke, his daughter, his angel.

Their family was now crowding Frimmke's parents' home. Menasheh's father found them a small dwelling on the outskirts of their neighborhood. Frimmke began creating a home for them, and Menasheh felt, more and more, like the matchmaker knew exactly what she was doing when she found them for each other.

This is where I am supposed to be, he thought one day in the market. *Now I am the one bickering with housewives over the prices of my beets, my chard, my leeks.*

But it wasn't where he was supposed to be. Only Moshe had an inkling of the great change awaiting them all.

Crystal

The other mystery gnawing at him lately, other than Uncle Julius, was the family crystal. Some of his earliest memories had to do with this collection of bowls, decanters, glasses of all sizes, other things he couldn't identify when he was small.

He first saw the crystal collection at his grandparents' house. Unfortunately (for him) as a kid he had a reputation for breaking things. Seems whatever he touched often fell and shattered, or fell and cracked, or fell and no longer worked. When the family visited his cousins on a Sunday, as soon as they saw him they'd run to their rooms and hide their toys. Even their comic books. One time he picked up a Superman comic and just flipping a page, it ripped in two. He would watch others play, or read, and he'd look at his hands, wondering what made them the enemy of anything fun.

More than once, if he was dragged with his mother

to visit some friend of hers, as soon as they walked in she would say, "Don't touch anything."

He was bad news, jinxed, or just unlucky.

His brother, however, was the opposite. He'd get his hands on anything, have a wild time with whatever he'd discovered, and then put back the artifact with only his fingerprint smudges to show it had been touched.

But the first time they came to visit their grandparents when the crystal was on display, his brother went too far. There was one piece, he was never sure what it was. It sat by itself in the den no one used, on the table where he saw the little candle burning for his unknown Uncle Julius. It was some kind of decanter, a something that poured something, with a fat flat bottom that kept it weighted on a table, and then curving thinner so it almost had a waist, and slightly expanding toward the top with a spout-like extension. And it had a top. All the glass intricately etched, shining like diamonds.

But the top was more impressive than the container it topped. It was probably twenty inches, starting with a sort of plug that went into the piece, to cap it and keep liquid from spilling out, then tapering far above into a thin sliver of glass, almost coming to a point. When removed, it looked like a sword from an alien race. The plug was obviously the handle, and when used as such a weapon, if it caught the sun, the room filled with rainbows that swooped around the walls.

That first time he saw it, he was so tempted to remove that top piece and just hold it in his hands. But he knew he was cursed, and by then had had enough experiences destroying stuff that he just stared at it longingly. However, Jake, as soon as he entered the room, went right to it, took off the top piece, and began swinging it around his head, causing those rainbows to fly around the room.

He didn't dare move, let alone breathe. He thought his brother was nuts, and felt that his good luck was finally going to turn. He could imagine the beating they'd both get; he'd be as guilty for letting his brother touch the thing, let alone swing it like a caveman's club.

His grandmother saw them in there, as she walked toward the kitchen. Her face changed, from questioning to rage to fear, in a second.

"What?! What did you do?"

She grabbed Jake's arm, the one holding the glass sword (he couldn't think of it in any other way, now), and he froze as if he'd been hit by a stun gun. She pulled it out of his hand, dropped his arm, then gently put it back into the decanter. Then it was as if he and his brother vanished because she paid them not a whit of attention. She ran her hands over the whole piece, now complete, unbroken, checking anyway, looking it up and down and around, keeping her hands on the sword longer than its body, checking, checking, confirming it was still in one piece.

And then it was as if he and his brother were suddenly there in the room again, flesh and blood.

"Out!" she screamed. He'd never heard his grandmother use this tone, and it scared the daylights out of him. "Get out! Now!"

They ran and didn't stop until they were in the backyard, barreling through rooms, exploding onto the back porch, flying down the stairs, finally hitting grass, out of breath.

"What the hell?" he said, giving his brother the stink-eye.

"I had to pick it up," Jake said, "didn't I?"

"And think you were Robin Hood?"

He didn't wait for an answer, but ran to the front of the house to sit on the stoop.

He wished he could've picked it up, but knew he'd drop it and get more than a yelling from his grandmother. She'd probably throw him out the window.

But he was now more than taken with this glass... whatever it was. What was it exactly? And where did it come from?

When he finally came back into the house, his parents and grandparents were sitting at the kitchen table having coffee. The anger of before was gone. The four of them sat, sipped, and chatted. His grandmother didn't give him a second glance as he walked by. He was heading back to the den, but no one seemed to care.

When he got there, thinking he'd more closely inspect the glass, its etching, just stare and be mesmerized by its size, its heft, its beauty, it was gone. The space where it was still had a doily on it, but it was like it never existed, and maybe he dreamt the whole thing. Jake found him there, staring at a blank space.

"What'd you do with it?" he said.

"This is because of you," he said, "it's gone because of you."

Years later, the glass piece returned, but not to the

den. Now it was in the living room, prominently displayed, with two other similar pieces on either side, making a trio of dazzle and sparkle. The first time he saw it again, he sat on the couch, and just stared and stared.

His mother caught him being hypnotized by its mystery, and she came and sat next to him.

"Aren't they beautiful?" she said.

"Jakie almost broke the sword that one time," he said, pointing.

He didn't know then, but found out years later, that his brother was also named for his Uncle Julius.

"These three," his mother said, "and the rest of the set, were in the wall of the laundry that Grandpa owned when I was a girl. He saw some loose bricks, and they came out so easily he knew it was a hiding place."

"The laundry I know?"

"You remember the laundry?"

His grandfather sold the laundry when he was five, maybe six.

"Sure, we'd go on Sunday before he took us to Coney Island. Jakie and I would go in the huge baskets and roll around like bumper cars."

"In the office, that tiny office, he took the bricks out and laid them on the floor. It was a hiding place, just like he thought. Inside there were packages made of newspaper, tied tightly. He took them out one by one. And in each package was a treasure. One by one he peeled away the paper, and he discovered this glass."

They both sat, staring at the treasure, or part of it.

"What was it doing in there? Who put it in there?"

She put her hand on his knee and gave him a gentle pat.

"That's enough questions for now. Remember not to touch."

And she left him there, with even more questions.

Becoming Max

Menasheh's son Moshe at first seemed to have the same gift he'd been given: a mind like a steel trap, where whatever came in would be saved forever, easily accessible. But once Menasheh taught him the most basic aleph-bet, the letters, and a few words, Moshe took the books they had in their home and curled up in his bed, reading for hours. One day he came to his father, and waited to be acknowledged.

"Yes, Moshe, what?"

"I need more books," the boy said.

"More books? We have books."

"I read them all."

His father wasn't expecting that. How had he read all the books? They didn't have many, but he hadn't even read them all. Some he'd never bothered to open.

"And I need more letters," Moshe said.

"I don't understand."

The boy scratched his head, trying to make clear

what he meant.

"You already know all the letters, especially if you've read all the books!" he said, laughing.

"No. I need more than Hebrew letters. I know there are other letters."

"What kind of letters are there?"

"The kind they read in America," he said, hoping he would be understood.

English? His son wanted to learn English? How would he accomplish this? Where would he find a book with English letters? He knew there was a small book shop in another part of town, but he'd never been there, and wasn't sure Jews were welcome.

But he'd try, for his son. So the next Shabbos, when the market was closed and most of the men were at synagogue, he told his wife he had an errand, and he walked for an hour to where he thought the shop was. He could feel the eyes of all the patrons turn to him, staring in an unwelcome manner, as he entered. He wanted to be in and then out as fast as he could.

An employee came right over, obviously wanting to help him get out quickly.

"Can I help the gentleman?" he asked in immaculate German.

"Yes, yes, please," he said, stammering in German, avoiding Yiddish. "For my son. A book. In English?"

"Right this way," the man said, as he followed him to another part of the shop. The man scanned a few shelves, took down two volumes.

"This is by Mr. Mark Twain, a famous American

writer. Your son would enjoy this book, I'm sure. And this one is by the revered William Shakespeare. It contains five of his plays."

The man didn't wait for Menasheh to say whether he wanted the books or not. He went to the front, wrote some numbers on a piece of paper, put the books in a bag, and handed both to Menasheh.

He knew not to say another word, so he took some bills from his pocket, counted out what was on the paper, handed the money over. The man put the cash into a drawer, then turned to help someone else.

Transaction over. He knew he needed to leave, so he was out on the street, it seemed, only minutes after he'd gone in.

He'd heard of Shakespeare. When he was a boy his father took him and his brother on a train to Hamburg. They saw a play in Yiddish that was written, in English of course, by Shakespeare. He didn't understand it, but was more taken with the train, and the fact that his mother allowed them to go. His father had relatives in Hamburg, and that was the pretext. Still, the theater experience, sitting in a darkened auditorium, full of strangers, while a make-believe world appeared on a stage, mesmerized him.

But Mark Twain was unknown to him. He flipped the pages as he got closer to his neighborhood, where he didn't feel as if he were being watched. The words were a mystery. How could he teach Moshe what they said? He had no idea how the boy would benefit from these two books.

He underestimated the gift his son had been given by God. When he gave the books to Moshe, the boy hugged him and wouldn't let go. Then he took the two books, went to his room, closed the door, and stayed there for the rest of the day. Menasheh had no idea how the boy would decipher anything in those pages, but before they were called to dinner, he came out with one of the books, and held it open for his father to see.

"Father, these words?" he said, pointing, "That is the name of the book. It says 'The Adventures of Tom Sawyer.' And here is the name of the man who wrote it, see? It says 'Mark Twain.' I can read these words!"

"How? How do you know this?"

"Every book has an author," the boy said. "Even the Torah, yes? So you told me the author of this one, and I knew that his name was Mark Twain and I knew his name would be on the first page. Then I find other words that have the same letters. You told me the name, the adventures of Tom Sawyer. Tom and Twain. The same sounds. It was like a puzzle. And you know how I love puzzles."

It didn't seem possible, but for weeks after school, his son would sit with these two books and wrestle with a foreign aleph-bet and figure out words and sounds, occasionally making marks in the margins of the pages. Now and then he would laugh to himself, as he read a page. Menasheh had to shake his head in disbelief. His son was learning to read another language, on his own.

His other two children had nothing like this gift. His younger son Shmuel was like any other boy, would rather play with rocks outside than study. His daughter Gdanke only wanted to be in the kitchen with her Mama, watching everything she did. Even at her young age she knew that one day she would be in charge of a household.

He thought that with these two books his son would settle into his life of school and study. It seemed like the family was solid in its existence. Menasheh went to the market in the mornings, working with his father-in-law, coming home as darkness fell, with fresh vegetables and the occasional chicken, or a few eggs. Life was good.

Then one day, a stranger appeared at the market. Menasheh had been trained to watch the people who crowded around the stalls. His father-in-law told him, you will see many you know. But when you see some you don't know, watch them carefully, in such a way that they don't know they are being watched. Most are harmless, passing through, needing some food for their journey. Some might be from the government, seeing that the correct tax was applied to whatever sold. But some want something for nothing, and they will use distraction to shove something within their coat. Or they will use confusion, as they ask questions while their partner takes what they need without paying.

Menasheh was good at this. He saw the stranger right away. The market was sparse on this morning; there were no crowds for a stranger to be lost in. The stranger stayed to the edges of the market, wearing clothes that looked hand tailored, and a hat Menasheh knew was expensive. And the man had no beard, which was an unusual sight. So he obviously did not live in this part of the city.

The man strolled around, looking here, looking there – for what, Menasheh could not figure. Then he stopped and reached into his coat. He took out a pouch of tobacco and commenced to roll a cigarette. As he licked the paper, after returning the pouch to his coat, that's when Menasheh knew. This was no stranger.

It was his old friend, Yakov. Or so he thought. Could it be? But as the man closed in on Menasheh's stall, smoking his cigarette, there could be no doubt. Here he was, standing before his old friend, looking at him with the same smile.

"Ah, Menasheh," he said, blowing smoke into the air, "I knew the matchmaker would find you the perfect match and you would make your place in our little world."

"Yakov?" He still could not believe this was his friend. "It is you?"

"Not bad, yes? I wear clothes I could never imagine when we were boys! This hat alone would have fed my family for a week! Ha!"

Menasheh's father-in-law, standing a distance away, had been watching this stranger interact with his son-in-law, and came over once they started talking.

"Menasheh, can I help?"

"Poppa," he said, "I must speak with this man, please."

Without waiting for an answer, he took off his apron, laid it on a crate of potatoes, and left the stall with the stranger.

Menasheh had never before left his father-in-law alone at the market in the middle of the day. The old man watched them walk off together, his mouth agape, while an old bubbe tried to get his attention.

"I don't like the look of these leeks!" she said, waving a stalk at the old man.

Although it was truly Menasheh's world, it felt like Yakov was leading him, not the other way around. Yakov brought them to a small café, ordered two coffees, paid for them, and led Menasheh to a table. Menasheh never came into this place. Why would he spend money on something he could get at home? He'd never been in a restaurant, and cafés were places for the idle rich.

"So, you are back after so many years," he said, and knew it sounded stupid as soon as he said it. He sipped the brew and thought it tasted burned.

Yakov was already smoking his second cigarette. He sipped the coffee as if it wasn't near to scalding.

"I live in Hamburg," he said. "The big city, yes? I ran away soon after we last spoke. I knew there was nothing for me here. I was wasting my time in that Yeshivah, the lessons fell off me like water falls off a duck. My poor mother rarely had enough food in our house to fill any of us. So I thought I would go and find my fortune."

"And have you?"

Yakov looked at him with eyes of mystery.

"Not exactly," he said. "For almost a year I lived on the streets, stealing food from carts, sometimes taking money from drunks without them even knowing. Yes, yes, my old friend, I see your face, I know it was bad. I see that you think I was bad, but I had to survive, and I did."

"But you don't live in the streets now, not with a hat like that."

Yakov took off his hat and blew some imaginary dust off its brim.

"That is correct, my friend. I finally was adopted.

Well, taken in, by a man who became my mentor. Who taught me the ways of the streets I had been struggling in. Who was part of a network of men who used that city in a way only the desperate do."

"You're a criminal," Menasheh said, not afraid of how Yakov would react. He expected some anger, or dismissal, or simple outrage, but Yakov laughed.

"I suppose I am," he said. "But my teacher taught me well, and I'm very good at what I do." He sipped his coffee, watching Menasheh, a sly smile showing his white teeth.

"Mazel tov," Menasheh said. "Is this why you came back here? To find me and tell me of your success?"

Yakov took the linen napkin, carefully wiping his lips. Menasheh had to admit, his friend had manners he never had when they were boys.

"Well, I suppose that's part of what I wanted to tell you. But I wanted to come back to see my old friend Menasheh one more time."

"One more time?"

"I'm leaving Hamburg. I have been given a very important job to do, one that will take me far from here. I'm going to America."

Menasheh almost choked on his last sip of the horrid brew.

"America?" he said.

"Can you believe it?" Yakov said, leaning in, whispering. "Could you ever imagine either of us making that journey across the ocean? To a new life?"

"What is this job that will take you to the new

world?"

"I have to escort a very valuable piece of cargo and never let it leave my sight."

Menasheh tried to understand. Nothing his friend said made sense.

"How valuable?"

"Listen, Menasheh, I just wanted to see you, sit with you a bit. Then I learned you had married, and have three children! And work in the market! Where I used to steal apples! I had to see for myself, take a last look at you, think of our old days, before I go and begin a new life."

"This cargo," Menasheh said, "I assume this is part of your criminal life?"

"This cargo will make my new life," Yakov said. "I will be a vital member in an operation that has been established in the great city of New York."

With that, Yakov stood, put his expensive hat on his head, came around the table, took Menasheh's face in his hands, and kissed him on both cheeks.

"Goodbye my friend, the only friend I ever had in this sorry place. I wish you only happiness, and peace, and many grandchildren!"

Before Menasheh could say his own goodbye, his friend was out the door, leaving him sitting there alone, with two empty coffee cups and a scrunched-up remainder of Yakov's cigarette.

Walking back to the market in a daze, Menasheh could hardly understand what had just happened. Was that really Yakov, a criminal living in Hamburg? Involved in some unnamed unlawful activity that was even more illegal than petty crime? That would take him to America for a life of even more horrific crimes?

Entering the stall, his father-in-law was waving his apron and scolding him without pause, but Menasheh hardly heard him as he took the apron, put it on, and began helping customers, almost shaking from the coffee he'd drunk with his old friend.

Menasheh walked home thinking of his youth, of the times he'd sat with Yakov arguing about the worth of their studies. Entering his house, it felt like he also brought in an uninvited guest, a certain sadness he'd never experienced before. *Is this my life?* he thought. *Arguing with old Jewish women about the ripeness of my tomatoes? Being berated by my father-in-law for taking coffee with a friend to break up my day?*

Hanging up his coat on the peg by the door, he noticed no smells from the kitchen. The house was sheathed in silence. Usually his children were playing in another room, often loud and boisterous, or else at least one of them running to greet him, with hugs and happiness.

Menasheh looked around, and by the fireplace his wife sat with the Rebbe of their synagogue. When she saw him, he couldn't figure out her expression. The Rebbe looked at him and beamed. Then he stood.

"And here is our proud Papa returning home from a hard day's work!" the Rebbe said, which made no sense. Menasheh was simply coming home as he always did, from another day like any other.

"Hello Rebbe," he said, adjusting his yarmulke on his head, even though he knew it needed no such adjusting.

"I was just saying, Frimmke, God sometimes comes to us, picks us up and carries us to a place we never imagined, and our lives open up like a flower in the sun."

Menasheh looked at his wife and he could see in her eyes that the Rebbe had just said no such thing to her. Then she looked into the fire, not taking her eyes away from the flames.

"Is that what God does?" he asked the Rebbe, who laughed in response.

The old man put his hands on Menasheh's shoulders.

"Sometimes, yes," he said. "I think, Menasheh, this is one of those times."

Frimmke got up from her chair without looking at her husband and went into the kitchen to begin chopping vegetables. The sound of her chopping was like a conversation she was having with him, without words. Chop! Chopchopchopchopchop. Chop! Chop! Chopchopchopchop. Chop!

"I don't understand, Rebbe."

The Rebbe sat and motioned for Menasheh to sit as well. He stroked his long grey beard, looking at Menasheh for a few breaths before he spoke.

"Menasheh, I have been instructed by our Glorious Rebbe in Hamburg to send a family from our congregation across the world, to help make a synagogue in another land."

"Across the world?"

"We are beginning a new chapter for our Hasidic brethren, and we will bring many of the old ways, to teach those who don't know, showing them how deep is our worship of Hashem."

"A new chapter?"

Chop! Chop! Chopchopchop! Chop chop!!

"You have a beautiful family," the Rebbe said. "Your son Moshe is the star of our Yeshivah, as you were too, might I remind you?"

"Thank you, Rebbe. We love our children."

Chop!

And then the chopping stopped, and Menasheh knew Frimmke was done arguing with her chopping. Now she was silent, so she could listen.

"We have discovered that you have a cousin who lives across the ocean! You know this, yes? Of course you do. So that is why I recommended you to our Head Rebbe. Isn't this wonderful? Your children will have opportunities they would never even dream of in our congregation! You will have a job waiting for you. Frimmke would be accepted into the sisterhood of a beautiful new synagogue."

"Are you sending us away?" Menasheh looked at the fire, but found no answers there.

The Rebbe stood up, wiping his hands as if he'd just done hours of manual labor.

"Whatever you cannot take with you, we will ship to your new home. The journey will take two weeks. We have your tickets, your passports, and we will give you some currency for when you arrive. You will need it to get off the ship and enter the city."

The Rebbe was already putting on his heavy coat.

"Wait, please," Menasheh said, "I still do not understand."

The Rebbe opened the door and before heading out,

he turned to Menasheh.

"This is a blessing," he said, "a gift from God. You leave in a week. Tell your father-in-law he will need to find someone else to help him in the market. We will bring you baggage for your clothing. And your tickets for the train to Hamburg, and the ship that you will board with your family."

And before Menasheh could say another word, the Rebbe was gone.

The next week was a dream within a dream. He thought about what the Rebbe had said, tried to pray for some guidance, but God was silent. On the night after being told his family was being sent to America, he sat after dinner watching Moshe read his English book by the fire. The boy's eyes were rapt; he did not blink even once.

"Are you liking your English book?" he asked his son.

The boy looked up.

"Yes, Papa," he said. "I am reading about a world I never knew existed!"

Before Menasheh could say anything, Moshe was back in his pages.

Watching his son read words that would always be foreign to him, Menasheh realized one thing the Rebbe said was true: this would be an opportunity for his children, even if it meant taking them away from everything they ever knew.

That night lying in bed, he told Frimmke that even though he could probably say no, they had to go. America was a chance they could never have chosen on their own.

They would never have been able to save enough to take their family on such a journey. It would be fraught with danger. But when they arrived, their lives would be so full of opportunity that their children would be blessed beyond their imaginings.

Although Frimmke made her best argument while the Rebbe explained the plan, with her chopping, she knew she had no power when it came to the synagogue. Their sect of Hasidism, which Menasheh subscribed to in the lightest of ways, had begun a community in America, and if they were told to go, they would go. She was, after all, a wife, and her job was to make a household and raise her children, no matter where that household happened to be.

Frimmke did her best to help the children understand what was about to happen. Only Moshe seemed to understand. She heard him one night explaining it to his sister Gdanke.

"We are going to take a trip on a boat, Gdanke," he said, "an adventure you will tell your grandchildren!"

"But I don't have grandchildren," the child said.

"But one day you will," her older brother said, "and they will be Americans."

No one came to say goodbye. Frimmke's parents were hurt deeply, and although they also knew there was no use arguing with the Rebbe, they did not want it to happen.

The children were obedient, and afraid, except Moshe, who'd packed his two English books in his small suitcase, and knew that where he was going, there would be thousands more, and he intended to read them all.

A train, where the children slept. Two parents taking

them to an unknown future.

A night in what would be a hotel for only the most downtrodden.

Crowds everywhere.

A ship larger than their whole town.

Then they were in the darkness of steerage, all five of them wrapped in fear, on a treacherous ocean.

Menasheh felt, with every day on the ship, that everything he knew, his whole life, was getting further and further away. He hardly talked. Frimmke barely moved from her bunk in steerage, where she held on to Gdanke and Shmuel with all her strength.

Frimmke refused to go upstairs and see the ocean, to walk the deck, to get some air. So he would bring his children, one at a time, while she stayed with them below. It was the day after a terrible storm, steerage had become more like Hell than the prison it had been, and he needed to breathe something other than the foul stench, so he told her he was taking Moshe upstairs for a break from the darkness.

The boy followed closely behind as they walked up the metal steps. Once on the deck, Menasheh breathed deeply. The sea was finally tranquil as the huge smokestacks threw out their black clouds.

From a distance he heard a commotion. The deck was crowded with steerage passengers, many smoking, children playing around the legs of their mothers. He heard a cry and then the commotion was coming their way.

He'd been aware of the criminals on the ship, who were probably given a ticket to rid their hometowns of their dark ways. At night he heard them working their way through steerage, fighting, drinking, stealing. Now it was coming closer to where they stood.

"Moshe," he said, "stay next to me. Don't move. Don't look at any of these men in the eyes."

Suddenly the prey of the gang was before them. A man with a bloodied face, eyes white with fear, looking at Menasheh with a pleading expression, but before he could speak, the thugs were upon him, beating, kicking, punching.

Yakov.

Menasheh was sure it was Yakov. What should he do? Yakov had begged with his eyes, but it was a quick second, then the gang commenced their punishment. Before he could even tell Moshe to look away, they picked up the bloodied soul and threw him over the side, into the ocean.

He took Moshe's head and turned him away, hugging him tightly. Once the gang realized they faced no threats from those on deck, they passed a bottle amongst themselves, drank, laughed, and went in the direction they'd come.

Menasheh looked into the water, but the ship was moving at such a pace he only saw the foam of the waves it created, and Yakov was nowhere in sight.

Menasheh was sick. He looked at the ground, couldn't look again into the dark waters, where his friend had just been thrown to his death. He took Moshe by the hand and led him back to steerage.

They'd walked a few yards and he saw, on the deck, off to the side, obviously stepped on, crushed by a horde of shoes, Yakov's beautiful hat he'd worn at the café. He pulled Moshe over to it, knelt down, picked it up, and stuffed it into the inner pocket of his coat.

When they finally reached the other side of the ocean, as they were preparing for their departure to the ferry that would take them to Ellis Island, standing with their meager luggage, Menasheh saw, untouched by anyone else, alone as if invisible, a wooden crate that seemed forgotten. And he knew, how he knew he had no idea, this is what the gang had been beating Yakov for – this is what they were after.

He pulled Moshe along leaving Frimmke with the children. He sat Moshe on the crate.

"You tell them this is ours," he said. "If they ask you what is inside, you say, gifts from my grandmother. You understand?"

The boy nodded, completely confused.

They dragged the crate with them onto the ferry, into the admissions at Ellis Island. He had no idea what was in the crate, but knew that Yakov was guarding it with his life, which he'd given. It had to be of value.

Making their way through the maze of immigrant admissions protocol, he felt more lost then ever. His son had taken charge, and he hadn't even noticed.

Here was Moshe, reading signs, telling them what lines to stand in. Here was Moshe, speaking with officials in a language he didn't understand.

Lines, lines, lines. From one to another. Whatever Moshe was saying, it was getting them closer to their new lives, and further from everything they knew.

He heard his son say something he knew to be wrong, even if he didn't understand the words.

"Julius," Moshe said, and then, pointing at him,

"Max," and pointing to his mother, "Dorothy," and his siblings, "Sam, Jenny."

They were suddenly out of the building, Moshe pulling the crate along the ground, Menasheh grasping for the other leather strap, toward another ferry.

"Moshe," he said, "what did you tell that man? Who is Max?"

Without looking back at his father, the boy said, "You are. And Mama is no longer Frimmke. She is Dorothy."

"I am not Max," he said, completely confused.

"You are now," Moshe said. "I had to give us American names that would be easy to write. Now take that hat you found on the boat out of your pocket, put it on, and throw your black hat away."

He did so. He felt like a fool with his thick black wool coat and a hat on his head that was worth a lot of money. He heard Shmuel laugh behind him; he managed a peek at his wife, who looked at him as if he were a stranger.

"Menasheh," she said, "what are you doing?"

"Max," he said to her, "you should call me Max now. Menasheh is back there, behind us, in Budapest."

"If you're Max," she sneered at him, "then who am I?"

"Dorothy," Moshe said to her, "but I think we should call you Dora. But I'll still call you Mama."

Heading to the island of Manhattan, his head full of noise, wearing the hat of his dead friend, Menasheh thought, for the first time, "I'm Max. Menasheh is dead, like Yakov. I'm Max."

Wrong Answers

When he finally got answers to questions about both his unknown Uncle Julius and the mysterious family crystal, he learned that almost everything he'd been told about both were either downright lies, evasions, cover-ups, or a kind of wishful make-believe.

His grandmother had a small breakfront with two glass shelves, and on those shelves were small pieces from the crystal glass set. Below these shelves were cabinets that he and his brother were allowed to explore. The bottom shelf had stacks and stacks of photographs, many held together with dried-out rubber bands, but many loose. His brother would go right to the top shelf, pull out small silver spoons, large bobs of thread from the laundry, and other bric-a-brac deemed safe enough for the two of them. But he was always drawn to the pictures, would take out a stack, pull off the rubber band, and lay them on the carpet, studying them, switching the order, shuffling them, without knowing who any of the people were.

Once, while exploring, he got to the stack that had one photo he'd never seen before. Laying them in a line on the carpet, they were black and white and from a time he knew was long ago. But there was one that was sort of brown and white. He picked it up, staring at the man staring back at him, with a smile on his face he couldn't quite figure out.

His mother was on the couch, reading the newspaper, while his grandmother worked in the kitchen, cutting up a chicken with butcher's shears. He took the photo over to her, holding it out.

"Why's it brown?" he said.

She took it and looked at it for what seemed a long time.

"This is Nana's brother," she whispered, so his grandmother wouldn't hear, "Uncle Julius."

"But Nana's brother is Uncle Sam," he said, confused.

"Yes, Uncle Sam," she said, "but there was another. He died a long time ago. Before I was born."

She handed him back the picture, meaning: end of discussion. He still didn't know why it was brown and not black and white like the other old ones. This was a few years after he'd first heard of this unknown uncle, the time he found the candle burning in the den. But he didn't remember that time. He was too young, barely came up to the table on which the candle burned, and that memory evaporated with time.

His Uncle Sam, he knew, wasn't his real uncle, but

his mother's uncle. He liked Uncle Sam. He would see him on the holidays when his family came to his grandparents' for dinner. His Uncle Sam had a wife he liked, too; her name was Rose. She had a wig she wore that was bright orange, and her cheeks always had a red circle in them that matched her lipstick, which often was put on so it covered more than her lips. His parents never liked his Aunt Rose (really his mother's Aunt Rose) and when he listened in on them one time talking about her, he heard the word "floozy" for the first time. He didn't know what a floozy was, but he loved the word. He would say it over and over while he colored in his coloring book, "floozy floozy floozy," and it made him laugh.

Now he learned that his Nana and her brother, his mother's Uncle Sam, had another brother, this guy in the brown picture. It didn't make sense. How come he died a long time ago, and why didn't they talk about him?

At the next holiday that included lots of extended family, it was probably Yom Kippur when everyone showed up at his grandparents' house to break the fast, he knew his mother's Uncle Sam and Aunt Rose, the floozy, would be there. He remembered the brown picture in the breakfront, and he wanted to show everyone that he knew a thing or two. He really wanted to ask Aunt Rose what a floozy was, but he thought it had something to do with dust bunnies, like he sometimes saw under his bed, and he wasn't quite sure how to frame the question.

So, instead, when the table was full of bagels and lox and herring and cream cheese and all kinds of other stuff, while there was a silence while the whole family chewed, he swallowed his bite, took a drink of milk, looked around at his cousins, his parents, his real aunts and uncles, his grandparents and his mother's Aunt Rose and Uncle Sam, and he said this:

"I know about Uncle Julius."

It was like the whole room froze in place. His mother gave him a look and his brother said loud enough so no one would miss a word, "Blake's in trouble now!"

His grandmother's face went sort of white. His mother's Uncle Sam wiped his mouth with a napkin and looked at him kindly.

"What do you know about him, Blake?" he said.

"He died," he said, and then thought, *am I in trouble?*

Uncle Sam looked at his grandmother, then his grandfather, then back at Blake.

"That's right, Blake, he died. At the start of a great war. He was a soldier. Did you know that?"

"Is that why he's wearing some kind of special clothes in the picture?"

Everyone watched this without moving. All eating stopped. He started to get nervous, but his mother's Uncle Sam smiled at him.

"That's called a uniform. Yes, that was his uniform in the army."

His grandmother looked at his mother.

"Where did he get that picture?" she said.

"It's with all the other pictures," he said, thinking this might keep him out of trouble.

"Do you want to know something else about him?" Uncle Sam said.

He nodded, and swallowed. He didn't think he should say anything right now.

His mother's Uncle Sam looked around the room. He saw his mother's Aunt Rose roll her eyes, and his grandmother gave her a look. He'd have to remember to ask his mother what a floozy was.

"He was my brother," said Uncle Sam, "and he saved this family. We wouldn't be here, right now, in this house, eating this food, if it wasn't for my brother, your mother's Uncle Julius."

He gave his grandmother a quick glance, and saw her wiping her eyes.

"Now let's finish this delicious food," Uncle Sam said, "and remember why we're here."

The next chance he got to look at that picture, he took that chance. For some reason his grandmother left it in the breakfront. He was sure she'd take it away like she'd done with the fancy crystal with the alien sword, but it was there on a Sunday when they came to visit his grandparents, which was a normal Sunday thing for his family.

His brother went to the stuff he normally took out, and started making a mess on the living room carpet with all kinds of junk, but he went right to the photographs.

It took him a while, but he found the picture. He lay on the floor, under a table that was high enough off the ground that he could sort of hide out there, and stared at the guy in the uniform who now had a name, Uncle Julius.

He liked him. His smile was welcoming, he stood tall and proud, then he realized that Uncle Julius was really smiling at the person taking the picture. But it was not the same as when someone took his picture and said, 'Say cheese.' No one said 'Say cheese' to this Uncle Julius. He knew this. He was smiling at the person holding the camera, in a way that showed a certain familiarity, but more than just a friend.

He flipped the picture over.

"My brother Julius" was written in a curly handwriting, in pencil. He did a quick calculation, and knew that whoever wrote this had to be either his grandmother, or his mother's Uncle Sam. That had to be who took the picture too, he figured.

The next time his family came to visit, he went right to the breakfront, like always, but when he opened the little doors, all the photographs were gone. That shelf was completely empty, except for a few broken rubber bands. He wished he'd taken the photo of Uncle Julius when he had the chance. He thought he'd never see it again.

But he was wrong. His grandmother, yes, had taken all those photos away so he wouldn't have access to them, but she put them in an album and put the album on a high shelf in her bedroom closet, out of reach. Years later, when his grandmother died, long after his grandfather was already gone, his mother inherited this album, and once again he was able to look at those ancient photos, and there was that sepia-toned picture of the long-gone Uncle Julius.

And eventually, he inherited the album from his mother. And then it was his, and he could finally find the answers that had eluded him for all those years.

Rose

Rose was always proud of the fact that she wasn't an immigrant, although her parents were. Born in Manhattan, her family lived for a while on the Lower East Side, until they were able to move to Brooklyn where it was less crowded, with many Jewish neighborhoods sprouting up in what had recently been farmland. Her father was a tailor, and all he needed was a good pair of scissors, a few spools of thread, needles, a measuring tape, and his eyesight. He found as many customers in Brooklyn as he had in Manhattan.

Her parents insisted she attend school. Rose learned fast and knew that the more she learned, the better her life would be. Being a girl meant no Hebrew school, no bar-mitzvah, just learning to cook, clean, and keep a house for a future husband, so school was a welcome refuge. She also liked books, and learning things about history, the history of this place she was growing up in. But as she got older, her mother tried to keep her home, saying, in many ways, you've had enough school, I need you here. But she managed to reach the 10th grade, with enough knowledge, she thought, to find some kind of job, somewhere.

In her neighborhood, like on the East Side when she was a girl, were many homes for immigrant girls and single women, called clubhouses. Civic and religious organizations created these residences; a way for women fresh to America to safely stay off the streets, possibly learn enough to work in a greengrocers, or an office, maybe a store, and hopefully find a husband. The Hannah Levinburg Home for Immigrant and Homeless Girls was only a few blocks from Rose's family's tenement, and when she was done with her schooling, her mother would let her go there now and then to keep her busy, and to get her out of the house, when it was so clear that Rose was tired of learning how to braid a challah.

The Levinburg clubhouse eventually opened up branches in the other boroughs, and many young women who started in Manhattan were sent to Brooklyn, or the Bronx, to fill those other rooms, and find work in other Jewish neighborhoods. The one that opened in Brooklyn was established with the help of a new synagogue. Rose's family, once they moved to Brooklyn, joined the synagogue, and Rose had a familiar place to go after school, to be away from her mother's kitchen.

This Levinburg clubhouse became like a second home to Rose. The upper floors were rooms for the immigrant women, but many neighborhood girls used the place as a way to make new friends, find some comfort in new relationships that were outside their immediate families, with no worries of strange men making advances. They were welcomed by the women in charge because the American girls would be teaching the new girls the ways of their new world, just by being with them.

The best part, though, for Rose, was not the socializing, although she made many friendships that lasted decades. On the first floor was a huge separate room that was used for neighborhood dances, where young men were invited to enjoy an evening of music, perhaps a small nosh, perhaps a drink, and the company of young lovelies who were eager to meet a man.

There was a player piano with rolls of the latest dance songs, and as long as someone could sit there pumping away, the music filled the room and couples could try out some of the latest steps. Sometimes someone had a banjo or a violin, and suddenly a home for immigrant single women became a dance hall, where the laughter of young people filled the air as couples danced new American dances, belonging in a way they never had before.

Rose looked forward to those dances like nothing else in her young life. To hear music played right there in that room gave her a thrill she'd never had before. After a few of those dances, it was all she looked forward to. She did manage to find a job in the neighborhood, doing light bookkeeping in the clothing store her father occasionally got work from, and it delighted her that she'd learned arithmetic, because it not only got her out of the house, it got her paid. She always gave half her earnings to her father, who let her keep the rest for whatever she wanted.

And she knew what she wanted: nice dresses to

wear to the Levinburg dance hall nights. And new shoes that would hold up to her ecstatic dancing.

She rarely danced with the young men who came to try and meet these girls. She had a few friends, two from her school, two she'd met when she'd helped out when the clubhouse had a Purim party, and the five of them would often get up together and dance, spinning with flying feet, while the rest of the crowd surrounded them, cheering them on, and bursting into applause when the song came to a raucous end.

She liked being watched by all the people. One of her girlfriends, also a native New Yorker, one night took Rose by the hand and led her out of the building. They walked hand-in-hand down the street, the music fading behind them.

"Rosie," her friend Esther said, "time for you to grow up."

"What are you saying?" she said, "I am eighteen!"

Esther reached into a pocket and took out a small metallic tube. Rose knew what this was.

"You have such a thing?" Esther said.

"No, but I'm ready."

"Okay," Esther said, "now hold still."

Esther held Rose's chin with one hand, and with the other lightly applied lipstick to Rose's face for the first time. Rose held her breath, excited to see her new face.

"Now," Esther said, smacking her lips, "do this, this, like this, yes." She took a tissue from inside her sleeve and showed Rose how to get any excess off her lips, and held up the tissue with red on it.

Rose did the same, and felt with her tongue her smooth American lips.

"Now this," Esther said, taking a cigarette from her small purse, "I show you how to leave your lips on the end of this," lighting it, inhaling, exhaling, and showing Rose the white end, now ringed with lipstick.

"I have to smoke?" Rose said.

"Only if you want!" Esther said, laughing. "The boys don't care if you smoke. They only want to see the red on the end, see? You can light one, hold it when you talk, make sure they see the red on the end, then put it in an ashtray. They have sisters at home, yes? Girls. They want to meet a woman. A man, he wants to meet a woman, not a girl. So, we go back, and maybe we find one!"

Esther took Rose's hand and led her back to the clubhouse. She wanted to get on that floor and make sure everyone saw her dancing with her new American lips.

The dances were only allowed to go until ten, and then all the local girls had to head home, all the Levinburg girls had to go up to their rooms, and the men were required to leave.

When Rose got inside, she expected to see a crowded dance floor, couples twirling and spinning to the music, but instead there was a crowd surrounding a man she hadn't seen before. Why wasn't everyone dancing? She inched her way through the couples and in the center of the circle was a short man, holding up something small.

"See?" he said, "how about this! A pen AND pencil set. This is the newest thing!"

The crowd oohed and aahed. Rose couldn't quite tell

what the excitement was. And then the man caught Rose's eye, and motioned with his hand to join him. Esther stood behind Rose and gave her a little push.

"Go see what he wants," Esther said, laughing.

"You know a pencil, yes?" the man said.

Rose wanted to be dancing, but she felt all the eyes on her, so she nodded her head.

"Of course, a pencil, who doesn't know a pencil?"

The crowd laughed, and Rose hoped her lipstick wasn't smudged.

"And you know a pen, yes?"

"Who doesn't know a pen?" she said, not to the man but to the crowd. Everyone laughed.

"Then I give this to you," the man said, handing her a small implement. "Now you have both, in one set!"

She looked at her hand. She'd never seen such a thing. He was right. There was a pen coming from one end and a pencil coming from the other. This was something.

He bowed before her and held out his hand.

"Sam," he said.

She reached out and shook his hand.

"Rose," she said, making a small curtsy.

"You can keep the pen and pencil set," he said, holding her hand. "Give it to your parents. They will be thrilled."

He held her hand up with his, like she'd just won a title fight, and said, "Now! Now we dance!"

The crowd cheered, someone new sat at the player piano, with new pep, and the music took off.

Couples peeled off the crowd and soon the floor was

filled with dancers, but Sam and Rose still stood next to each other. She held the small pen and pencil combo, not sure where to put it.

"Let me," Sam said, taking it and putting it in his suit jacket's pocket. "I will remember to give it to you later, on our walk home. Now, can you dance?"

He gave her a smile that was more a question, and this time he held out his hand not knowing if she would take it. But she did, and since the Levinburg was a place of such familiarity and comfort for Rose, she led him to the middle of the dance floor, and allowed his arm to surround her waist while his hand took hers, and they spun to the music, and Rose felt like she was floating above the floor.

They danced the next three songs. Rose didn't want to stop, but her feet were killing her, so before the next one started, she said, "Maybe some water now," and led Sam to the far wall, where there were refreshments.

Esther was on the dance floor with their other girlfriends, and she gave Rose a thumbs up, but Rose wasn't exactly sure what that meant. Sure, she had a man, and they were now sipping water, but did that mean anything?

"You live upstairs?" Sam said.

"Me? No. No. I live with my family, here in the neighborhood. I live here, I work here."

"Ah," he said, "so you are not an immigrant, like me?"

"Like you? No. I was born in Manhattan. My parents, they came over. I was born here."

The music suddenly stopped, and the matron of the house, as she was called, rang a small bell.

"Okay," the matron said, "ten o'clock! Everyone out! All my girls, upstairs! Thank you for coming, everyone! Good night!"

"She's not very friendly," Sam said.

Rose took his glass and hers and put them on a table.

"We have to go," she said, leading him toward the door.

"Can I walk you home?" he said.

"Me? Walk me home?"

He padded his jacket.

"I still have your pen and pencil set."

She laughed, taking his hand.

"Sam," she said, liking the sound of his name coming from her lips, "yes, you can walk me home."

It was a short walk, just a few blocks, but they held hands the whole time. Rose had never held any man's hand, other than her father's. They talked about their lives. Sam told her he'd come over as a young boy, with his brother and sister and parents. Now it was just his sister at home, with their parents. His brother died in the epidemic. Rose didn't know what to say. None of her family had gotten sick.

"That is terrible," she managed to say.

Sam shrugged, looking at the sidewalk, avoiding her eyes.

"God gives to us," he said, "and God takes away, too."

Rose stopped walking, and faced Sam.

"Did I say something bad?" he said.

She put her hands on his shoulders.

"No, Sam," she said, "but we're here. I'm home."

"Oh, oh," he said, "you're home."

They stood facing each other. Then his eyes lit up and he reached into his jacket.

"Give this to your father," he said, handing her the pen and pencil set. "He will think you came from the future!"

She took it, nodded, and smiled.

"The future," she said.

"Will you be at the next dance?" he said.

"Yes," she said. "Will I see you there?"

"If you're there, I'm there," he said reaching over, kissing her cheek.

He headed in the other direction, but turned back to her as she stepped onto the front stoop. "And we'll dance!" he said.

"We'll dance!" she said, waving goodnight.

Rose knew her mother was watching from a window. She always was there, waiting for Rose to safely walk through the door. But tonight she had a few words, and Rose knew they were coming.

"A man?" her mother said as soon as she opened the door.

"Sam," she said, handing over the pen and pencil set.

Her mother looked at the thing she'd been given, turning it this way and that.

"What is this? Who is Sam?"

"That," Rose said, sitting at the kitchen table, "is a gift from Sam, and it is from the future, Mama!"

"There is no such thing," her mother said.

"Look, see? A pencil on one end, and look! A pen on the other end!"

"That is ridiculous," her mother said, putting it on the table. "Who is this Sam?"

It took Rose a few more dances to truly find the answer, but she loved every minute of being with her new friend. She bought her own lipstick, and would spend more time getting ready for each dance than she did before. She didn't think she was on a real date when she was with Sam, but Esther told her that's what it was. She was only with Sam, Sam was only with her, she couldn't wait to see him, and he couldn't wait to dance with her. What else would you call it?

"So after tonight," Esther said, "you say that next time, he doesn't meet you here, next time he picks you up!"

"Picks me up?"

"At your house, Rose."

"But he would have to meet my mother!"

"He'll have to meet her eventually, yes?"

"Yes, he will."

"The dance after next, it's Purim, okay? Everyone will be at the dance. So next time he walks you home, you say, Sam, you come get me for the Purim dance. We don't meet at Levinburg. You come to my house. And when he knocks on the door, you say that before you go to the dance, he has to come in and have some of your Mama's latkes that she makes for Purim."

"I do?"

"Yes, mamaleh," Esther said. "He will love your

Mama's latkes."

"They're very good," Rose said.

"And what did your Mama always say?"

Rose smiled at the memory.

"She always said, my latkes are so good they are not just for Chanukah!"

Esther laughed.

"Yes! Latkes for Purim? We never heard of such a thing. What, my mama once said, she can't just make hamentashen like everyone else?"

Rose only thought of the next dance as a way to get to the one after, so although she had a great time with Sam, he found her distracted. Walking home, now hand in hand, he thought it must have been something he did.

"I'm sorry," he said, approaching her street. They'd hardly talked the whole way.

"What are you sorry for?" she said.

"Whatever it is I did to make you seem so far away."

They stood at the bottom of her stoop. She could feel her Mama's eyes on them, staring from behind a curtain.

"Sam," she said, "next time, we don't meet at Levinburg. Next time I wait for you here."

"Here?" He didn't quite understand. He hoped he did, but he wasn't sure.

"Here," she said, pointing to the front door, "there. Next time I wait for you, and you come here, and you take me to Levinburg."

He looked at the door, he measured the steps in his mind, he looked back at the door, and he saw Rose's mother for a brief second as she hid her face behind the curtain.

Sam waved.

"Who are you waving at?" Rose said, searching the windows.

"Your Mama, I think," he said, facing her. "I don't think she likes me."

Rose reached up and kissed him on the cheek.

"Sam," she said, squeezing his hands, "she doesn't know you. Next time, okay? Remember. You come get me."

"I will come and knock on the door," he said.

"That's right," she said, turning and heading up the steps.

He watched her until the door closed and he was left standing alone. He'd never picked up a girl before to take anywhere. He couldn't wait.

But he had to. During the next week, during whatever he was doing, brushing his teeth, walking to his job, eating dinner with his sister and parents, he imagined Rose doing it too. Looking in the mirror, his mouth foamy with toothpaste, he thought, she's looking at herself, while she brushes. Maybe she uses a powder, maybe she uses Pepsodent. A hundred times a day he'd think, maybe she's drinking water too, right now, at her own sink, maybe she's asking her Mama how her day was.

All those tricks didn't make the next week come any faster. But suddenly, as if the previous week didn't even exist, Sam stood at Rose's door, knowing she was inside, waiting for his knock.

He'd barely raised his hand when the door opened, and there she was.

"You said I was to knock," he said.

"Yes, yes," she said, pulling him inside.

"But I didn't have a chance," he said, as she closed the door behind them.

"You were going to knock, I saw you," she said, as he hung his hat on a small hook on the wall.

He smiled.

"You saw me," he said, laughing, "but you didn't let me."

She took his arm and led him to a door down the hall. This tenement had two apartments on each floor, like so many others in the neighborhood. Where they were now was the hallway where tenants hung coats, took off wet shoes to dry, where neighbors saw each other in their coming and going.

"That was good enough," she said, opening the door to their apartment.

It wasn't so different from where he lived, a tiny kitchen with barely room to stand, a table with four chairs in another tiny room, where they stood, a small square space from where he could see both kitchen and dining room, and a small hallway down where he knew were bedrooms and a minuscule bathroom. Rose's mother stood in the kitchen; her father sat at the table, his eyes on a newspaper. He didn't look up.

"Daddy," she said, in a voice he hadn't heard before, "this is Sam."

The old man looked up, nodded his head. "Sam," he said, and he was back to reading.

"Come," Rose said, leading him to the kitchen. Her mother stood over a stove, the sound of latkes frying making Sam's mouth water. "Mama, here is Sam."

The woman looked up from her frying.

"You want a latke?" she said, putting one on a plate crowded with the little potato pancakes.

"I do like them," Sam said. He gave Rose a quick glance and in his eyes she knew he was saying, why latkes? It's Purim!

"Come, sit," Rose said, taking his hand.

He hated to admit it, but Rose's mother's latkes were better than his own mother's, who he always thought was probably the best cook he knew. He sat with her family, and they ate quietly, Sam made sure not to drink his water too loudly. He mostly stared at his plate, and when he looked up for a quick second, both Rose's parents were not eating, but looking at him.

"These, these are delicious," he said.

Rose's mother shrugged.

"I burned the oil," she said.

"Mama! You did no such thing!" Rose said.

"Well, they are still delicious," he said, giving Rose a quick wink. "I don't even want the applesauce, or the sour cream."

He thought he could see a smile out of the old woman, that she was trying to stifle.

"Well," she said, giving him a quick glance, as she put a latke on her plate, "then you can have another if you would like."

Rose knew this meant acceptance.

The next dances were more and more like dates. Sam always picked up Rose and walked her home. They always held each other's hands, and there was the kiss on the cheek standing in front of Rose's tenement. Sam would try to catch her mother peeking through the curtains, and when he did see her attempting to hide away, he lifted his hat, calling out, "Good evening, Mama! I brought Rose home, safe and sound!"

"Sam!" Rose would say, laughing, "stop."

"Safe and sound," he'd call out, as Rose opened her front door, "see? Here she comes! You can ask her yourself!"

They were married six months later.

Becoming Sam

Yesterday was Georgie's funeral. This I can't believe. Rose and I walked into the funeral parlor and saw Georgie's kid sitting off to one side, looking lost. I could tell that the weight of the whole thing was on him. Why didn't anyone tell me Georgie was sick? I approached him and saw the boy I once had a catch with on a Thanksgiving day. Now all grown. Jimmy, I think he's called. I told him he wouldn't remember me, that I was a friend of his father's from the old neighborhood, that his father took me to Coney Island for the first time. He looked at me like I was speaking Russian, didn't hear a word.

His sister, Adra, she remembered. "Hi, Sam, so good to see you," she said, through tears. We hugged and I sat with them while Rose mingled, looking for familiar faces. Then we followed in the line of cars to the cemetery. I watched while they lowered my oldest and best friend into the ground. On the ride home, myself in tears so I almost crashed the car, I thought about that day so many years ago, and it seems like yesterday.

Georgie, he was the one who made me feel like an American and not like the child of immigrants, standing outside, looking in, like my folks. He showed me the ropes. How can you thank someone for being that kind of friend? You can't.

My older brother Julie, he tried to, but he was gone so quick. I barely remember the boat, but I remember Julie in the dark of the steerage, holding my hand. I remember how, once we got to New York, he took charge because my parents were too frozen with fear. Julie spoke English and we followed him blindly as he managed to get us off the boat, through the Ellis Island, onto a ferry, into Manhattan, and eventually, through streets crowded with noise, to the underground train that took us to Brooklyn, where he even managed to get us into a taxi, something then I could never even imagine, to a cousin he had an address for.

The whole time he and my father lugged a crate that we hadn't started out with, that somehow became ours on the boat. It was wood, it had two straps, and my father never took his grip off one, and Julie had the other when it needed to be moved, lifted, dragged. Once we got to the house in Brooklyn, that crate was lugged up a flight of stone steps into the front room. My father finally looked relieved of it. Then I saw my father weep for the first time, as his cousin grabbed him, and they hugged long and hard, my father howling with tears while my mother watched, mouth open in shock.

Georgie was my best friend, because he took me

and taught me and accepted me. And now he's gone and I'm an old man, but what can I tell you? It seems like yesterday.

Georgie got me talking English like a Brooklyn kid though I still heard the other kind of talking, the Yiddish, but I didn't remember it much. My folks always talked what I used to call the old talk. When we first came here I didn't speak no American, but I learned fast. Seems that as soon as I learned it I forgot the other.

Georgie would say, no Sam, not like that, like this, and he'd practice with me in the schoolyard, where I was forced to go while my sister stayed home and Julius looked for work. And then Julius ended up in the army, and that's where it all went bad.

I liked the school, because it was warm and where we lived it was mostly cold. Some days Mama was crying when I came home. She'd be sitting in the kitchen, crying so soft. She'd see me and grab me and hug me so hard I thought I'd break. My Pop worked on Pitkin Avenue, in a shoe store, where other Jews came in so he could talk Yiddish and still make some money, and I'd see him sometimes after school. He worked with Benny Steffens, who was Georgie's pop.

At school we were allowed to go into the yard and do whatever we wanted. I mostly hung with Georgie. He not only helped me talk good but also showed me how to smoke. This one time he took out his pack, gave me an Old Gold. I never smoked before so first I coughed, but then it went down easier. I didn't feel my tongue for a while and thought I was going to throw up, but after that went away I liked it.

After school, walking home, Georgie said, "You

ever get the strap?" and I said no. He pulled out a little box and said, "You better take one of these." It was Sen-Sen.

"What's this for?" I said.

"It's so your folks don't smell the smokes on ya breath."

When I'd come home my Mama always made me wash my hands. She'd yell at me, "You're going to put food to your mouth!" But that day I had my first smokes I went to the bathroom and when I turned on the water it smelled like I had just had one. I took Sen-Sen so I knew it wasn't on my face. Where could the smell be? Then I knew: my hands. They smelled just like Georgie's Old Golds. So I washed my hands real good and then I made sure to wash them everyday without being asked.

I'd never heard of Coney Island, and Georgie had the idea to take me long before we ever went. He had a plan. It started on a Sunday. My Pop worked Sunday with Benny, and my Mama would spend the day cleaning the place and I always knew we would have a good supper if she bought a chicken. This one Sunday Georgie came by to see if I could come out, and she let me go.

First we went to the roof for my smokes which I kept hidden there. We started out on Belmont Avenue, where the pushcarts were. I always liked Belmont 'cause of all the noise. If we moved fast through the crowds I usually came away with something. I'd swipe an apple off a cart and the guy wouldn't even look my way. Georgie taught me that too, and said, this means you belong here. Then Georgie said, "We need to get you some money, Sam."

We went over to Rutland Road, about five blocks

from us. I'd never been on this street before. Georgie stopped by one house and sat on the stoop. He pointed across the street with his eyes.

We watched people go out of their houses and come back in again. Just then he pointed down the street and I saw a cab coming our way. There was a lady in the back seat.

"Okay," he said, pulling two yarmulkes out of his pocket, "put this on."

"This? I don't wear these beanies, except at Passover. What's the joke, Georgie, huh?"

"Put it on and let me do the talking." He stuck it on his head, and I did likewise. Then he got up and we walked over to the cab as it pulled to the curb. An old lady got out, and I could see that the back seat was full of paper bags.

"Need some help, Mrs. Rapkin?" Georgie asked the lady.

"Yes, Georgie, please. Your friend can help, too."

We started pulling bags out of the cab. When we finished, we stood in the lady's kitchen. I had no idea what we was waiting for.

"This is for you, Georgie," she said, opening her purse. She took out a small pouch. I could hear the money jingling. She gave Georgie a shiny new quarter. I couldn't believe it! Then she looked at me.

"And this is for you." She handed me a dime. "You're such good boys."

Georgie said thanks and I just smiled, clutching my dime. We ran down to the street. We had 35 cents between us!

"Who was that lady, anyway?"

"She knows my ma. I was here once and I helped her and she gave me a dime. Next time it was a quarter. If we time it right, we can be here when she comes home. And she'll always give us a quarter."

I was itching to head back to Belmont and get a knish, but Georgie told me I should keep the dime, and hide it with my smokes. He said every time we helped Mrs. Rapkin I should keep the money and never spend it.

This was all part of his plan that I didn't know about.

That night, after I went home and we had our chicken, I went out on the fire escape to watch the cars. I took out my dime to look at it. I remember how the lady on the dime looked so pretty with the wings in her hair.

After a few months I had saved $1.50. I never thought I'd have so much money. I figured I should give some to my Mama but Georgie told me not to. "She won't believe you when you tell her where you got it," he said, "and she'll make you give it all to her. Then you'll get the strap." So I didn't, but I wanted to.

One Sunday Georgie came to my house as usual, and I had on my good shirt so we could go to Mrs. Rapkin's and get our quarters. But instead he pushed me into my room and shut the door.

"Get your money," he said, "and your smokes. Today's the day."

We walked over to St. John's Place and took the trolley down to Franklin Avenue. We dropped our nickels in and Georgie asked for two transfers. At Franklin we got off and walked to the elevator trains. When the train got to Stillwell Avenue, I could see the wonder wheel in the distance and I knew: this was Coney Island! The train stopped and we ran down to the street.

All the guys at school had been to Coney but never me. My pop didn't think it was a good place for Jewish folks to go. But Georgie had been, with his folks, and he told me about it. He told me that there was all kinds of things to do there that his folks wouldn't let him do. He said that one day he would take off and go all by himself. And I guess this was the day, only he wasn't all by himself, he was taking me.

The streets was crowded with people. I was ready for anything.

We went to Nathan's, and had hot dogs for a nickel apiece, washed down with orange sodas. Then we hung on the side streets for a while, where we went into the penny arcades. First we played skeeball. You got nine balls for a nickel, which seemed like a good deal. Georgie made it look easy but I tried it and couldn't get more than 20. There was one guy, a sailor, with tattoos on his arms, and he was the best. His girlfriend hung on his arm. Her lips were painted red, and when I met my Rose I remembered this woman I'd seen at my first penny arcade. We watched him for a while to see how he did it. He winked at me and said, "Watch this, kid," and got a bullseye!

Then we tried more stuff. For a dime you got three baseballs and had to knock down a pyramid of six bottles, but that didn't work. Georgie tried a rifle range and for a quarter he got 15 shots, but he didn't hit anything. I tried a gun that shot water, and I almost won a bamboo cane, but didn't. If we weren't careful, we'd be broke in no time.

After another hot dog and more cotton candy, Georgie said, "Let's hit the Cyclone." Now I had heard of the Cyclone, cause every kid at school who'd been to Coney rode it, so I thought I could too.

Everyone on the ride was screaming. I heard one kid crying for his life. When we got on, I thought I was ready, but I wasn't. I kept my eyes closed, but Georgie punched me when he saw me, so I had to watch everything. The guy in front of me threw up and it sprayed back and hit me, and I thought I'd do the same to the guy behind me, but I was too busy screaming. I don't know how we didn't get killed, but Georgie told me that no one was killed yet, and after it was over, they was loading it up again to take another bunch up there to scare the pants off them, too.

It was wall-to-wall people now, everywhere. Georgie pulled me to a side street where there was gypsy tea rooms and fortune tellers. He gave me a smoke. I needed it after the Cyclone.

"Let's go get some hot dogs," I said to Georgie.

"Nah, let's go to Steeplechase."

I seen the horses going all around the outside of Steeplechase, up in the air. Not as crazy as the Cyclone, but a good view. So we each got on our mechanical horse and pretended we were at the races, riding around the whole Steeplechase, looking down at all the people. When we finished we got off and there was two ramps. A guy sort of pushed us on one ramp. We went through a maze that had barrels on the floor and it was hard to walk on, but we made it through. Then we were in the audience, looking at people coming through the other ramp, up on a stage.

"Watch this," Georgie said.

A couple came through. On the stage was a house, huge playing cards painted all crazy, a tree with hot-dog branches, and a doghouse. There was a midget clown and a cowboy leading them through, and a farmer too.

When the lady walked through, the farmer pulled out a telescope and yanked it open, looking at the lady's legs. The audience whooped it up at that. The clown started jumping up and down near the footlights, shaping with his hands, double barreled curves, his eyebrows going up and down. He meant the lady.

Now the cowboy and the farmer turned on the two of them, almost pushing them down to the stage, near a pink elephant with yellow tusks. These two had no choice. They had to go through the exit sign. The cowboy looked at their tickets again, and all of a sudden a blast of air pours up through the floor, and the lady's skirt is yanked up around her head!

Me and Georgie nearly peed our pants. Then the cowboy looks at us and says, "She got a good airing!" Just as you'd think the boyfriend would get mad at all this stuff, the farmer dropped to the ground and picked up a strange stick laying there. He reached out and touched the rear of the boyfriend, and it stung him!

By now Georgie and me was having a pisser watching all this. Then the clown grabbed the girl and led her by another blast of air, and up goes her dress around her head again. "A good blow!" he yells, and the audience is going nuts. The eye of the elephant turned red, and we was all laughing hysterical. The couple was led to one more blast of air, and then into the audience. And the whole thing started again.

We counted up our money, and Georgie figured that we had enough to still go to Luna Park. That was the best at night, he said. So after we split a knish we headed for Luna, just as the lights was coming on.

It was like a city of fire rising from the ocean to the sky. Hundreds of towers, like Chinese style, all lit up and glowing. It was more light bulbs than I ever thought could be in one place. There was lots inside Luna Park that we didn't care about, like the Tunnel of Love, but we rode more rides and walked around looking at all the lights.

I was getting tired but Georgie said that we had to see one more thing. We had enough plus our nickels to get us back to the neighborhood, so Georgie took me into the tiny hospital to see the baby incubators. I didn't know what a incubator was but Georgie said I would find out. The place looked like a hospital, there was nurses walking around and it was very quiet. This was no ride and I don't think it was a freak show neither.

Then a guy walked out and started telling us about the preemies. Behind a glass window was these tiny glass cases and there was a baby in each one, at least it looked like a baby. Then these nurses took them out and each nurse had one in each hand and held them up. They looked like the salamis hanging in the butcher shop, all red and tiny. How could they be so small? The guy was telling us about Dr. Couny, who invented these things, and how he keeps them at Luna Park cause no hospital would have them.

The guy said that one of the nurses holding two of these preemies was herself a preemie twenty years ago right here at Luna Park and now she was back taking care of all the other preemies. He told us all about how when there was a fire at Dreamland, a place at Coney Island that ain't there no more, they had to rescue the preemies from there and that's when they moved back to Luna.

I remembered hearing my folks talking one night about "the baby" and I didn't know what they meant, 'cause my sister was the baby, I was in the middle, and Julie was the oldest. Suddenly I remembered more, when my mama started crying. I got chills thinking that I would have had another brother or sister but it died.

After we finished there, we headed for the trains. When the trolley came by our stop we must have fallen asleep, cause suddenly I opened my eyes and we were past it. We had to backtrack. By the time we were in the neighborhood, there was no other kids on the streets. Walking on Pitkin Avenue I seen the light on in the window of our pops' store, which should have been dark by then.

"Ain't that unusual, huh Georgie?" I said.

We snuck up to the window. The light was on but we didn't see no one. Why had my Pop and Benny forgot to turn the lights off? Then Georgie slugged me and screamed, "Look!" Through the curtain that led to the back room, I saw some legs on the floor. It was my Pop! He was moving around and I could see his legs tied up! It was a robbery!

Georgie ran to Barney's corner candy store and screamed at Barney to call the cops, cause our pops was tied up in the shoe store. I started shaking all over needing a smoke, but I knew I shouldn't, so I just swiped some candy when Barney ran out to wait for the cops. Pretty soon we heard the sirens and three cars pulled up, their red lights blinking. One cop busted the door open and we was right: My Pop and Benny was both tied up.

The cops started shooting questions at Benny, and it sounded like the stick-up just happened. One of the coppers went to call it in. Me and Georgie saved the day, and we knew that with all the excitement it would be a while before our pops figured out that we shouldn't have been out so late in the first place.

"These youngsters are responsible for us getting here, Mr. Steffens," one of the coppers said to Benny.

My Pop looked down at me and I could see how scared he was now that it was all over. I ran over to him and hugged him hard, and he hugged me back, which surprised me, cause he never did that before.

"You're a good boy, Sam," he said.

After the cops talked to Benny and my Pop some more, they said that they was finished and we could go home. Benny closed the lights, locked the door, pulled the gate down, and we walked for a few blocks with Georgie and Benny until we got to our building.

My Mama was on the front stoop, with a bunch of the ladies, all talking and worried. When they seen us coming, my Mama screamed and threw her hands in the air. She started yelling at my Pop in the talk I didn't understand, and for a while I got lost in the shuffle.

That was my chance to run upstairs, wash my hands, and eat some Sen-Sen. I knew I stunk like cigarettes. But just as I was turning on the water, my Pop walked in behind me, and grabbed the soap out of my hands. He looked at me and all that about us saving the day seemed to disappear.

"What did you do?" he screamed, and he pulled me out of the bathroom before I could tell him anything. I don't know what I would have told him anyhow, cause nothing would have sounded good, even to me. He kept screaming, "Cigarettes?? You smell like cigarettes?" Now he was crazy and I was scared for a second. He yanked off his belt and for the first time I got it just like Georgie said I would. He whipped me good, chasing me from room to room, then I was back in the bathroom and he slammed the door on me and just kept screaming and hollering and whipped me until I couldn't tell him not to no more. Then he walked out and left me there, on the floor.

I knew if Julie was still here, none of that would've happened. I knew it.

I heard him go into the kitchen and open the window box. He took out the leftover Passover wine and I could tell he was taking a glass from the sink and then he opened the bottle. It sounded like he poured out a lot. Then he shot a shpritz of seltzer in the wine and I heard him drink. I was laying on the bathroom floor afraid to move.

When my Mama came upstairs she saw him and then they was both crying and talking the other talk again. I didn't know what was going on. I heard him say, "They will come back," as I got up to wash my face, quiet as a mouse, and then got into bed.

I wished I could tell Julie about my day, but he was so long gone. I did have his picture, so I took that out and sort of told him about it, in my head. It wasn't the same as him being here, but I could tell he was listening, smiling at me. My sister slept even though I had the light on. I grabbed a pencil, and on the back of the picture I wrote, "My brother Julius," and then I put the picture in my secret shoe box, turned off the lights, and tried to sleep.

But I knew I saved the day. And I knew that now I was a real American 'cause I went to Coney Island. And I forgave my Pop for giving me the strap because I knew that he would never be no American. He would always just be someone right off the boat.

And I had Georgie to thank for that day, and I'll never forget him for it.

Blake

When Blake's father died, he'd already moved out west, and Jake had already sent him the tape with the only recording of his parents' voices. He hadn't yet begun his search for the answers that eventually nagged him: the true origin and importance of the family crystal, and the truth about his long-dead great-uncle who died in the 1918 flu epidemic.

He'd been raised Jewish, but his family was truly secular. They belonged to a synagogue but only as a vehicle for his mother's desire to be part of the Sisterhood, a group of white Jewish middle-class women who occasionally participated in vaguely philanthropic pursuits; and as a way, he finally came to believe, for his father to feel freed from vague notions of sin stemming from his life of religious exile.

He and Jake had had Hebrew school forced on them when they turned about eight, in preparation for their bar-mitzvahs, which would happen five years later. Blake tried to fight this, his first attempt to challenge the authority of his parents, but came to realize that at that age, he'd be lucky to extend the time he could stay up watching TV. Jake saw the battle as futile from the start, after watching Blake's failure, so he simply went and hated yet another school, three days a week, after public school. But for Blake, his attendance signified not only his first loss to his parents' – really his father's – bidding, but the realization that his going was a way for his father to feel less guilty about his own choices.

His father, Blake's paternal grandfather, wasn't particularly religious, but as a child of immigrants of that early 20th century generation, it was strictly forbidden to advertise one's departure from decades of observance and belief. Blake's father, on the other hand, made it clear that if he belonged to a synagogue, paid for a seat on the High Holy Days, sent his sons to Hebrew school, and had them bar-mitzvahed, he could work on Saturday, drink when he wanted to, and pretty much ignore anything having to do with being an observant Jew.

His mother, on the other hand, came from more religious stock. Her parents, who also came over as children on the perilous journey from Eastern Europe, clung to their religion as a safety net when needed, a life preserver when threatened, and a way to create a nurturing household in a new and dangerous world they never worked at fitting into. And when his grandmother lost her older brother in the flu epidemic, just a few years after their arrival, it was religion that gave the family a way to survive, with rituals and comfort that allowed them to properly mourn, release their grief, and carry on.

Blake came to believe, as he went through the rigmarole of religious training, that his years of education, ultimately, had little or nothing to do with him. He slogged through learning the hieroglyphs of Hebrew, until the ancient letters actually made sense. But he liked the fact that he could read something his father could not. He tried to fight the other rituals foisted on him: the prayers, the structure of a Shabbat service he was forced to attend, and the many holidays along with their own specific services, prayers, histories, and places in the Jewish calendar. But he lost those battles, one after the other.

It was when he was coming to the last lap of his Hebrew education, the actual preparation for his bar-mitzvah, that the true reasons for these years of hated turmoil started to become clear. At first he thought it was because his mother had wanted her sons to follow in the footsteps of her parents and grandparents, and have some piety in their lives (and hopefully, he later understood, marry Jewish women), which would somehow – though he never understood how – make them better men.

But as he started his actual lessons for his rite of passage, the learning of his Torah portion, the specific blessings he'd be singing on his bar-mitzvah day, and especially the ritual of the phylacteries, the T'fillin, it truly came clear. He was having the bar-mitzvah his father never had. He was clearing that specific sin off his father's slate. He was making a correction to a mistake that was not his.

When he learned the Kaddish, the prayer for the dead, his twelve-year-old brain finally connected enough of the dots that he truly got it. His father was not only using him to absolve him of his father's sin of depriving his son of a true Jewish life, but he was insuring that, upon his death, whenever that happened, his son, Blake, would insure a proper Jewish afterlife by reciting the prayer that would allow him to pass over into whatever Jewish afterlife there was.

This realization came slowly. It seemed like one more useless lesson for something he'd never use, once he was old enough to reject it. He hated his teacher, who never gave him – or any of the boys in his class – any praise for accomplishing all these extra tasks, but he also hated that this prayer was never translated for him. By the time of his lessons he understood a bit of Hebrew, but this prayer was gibberish. It was only required. He had to learn it. No arguments.

Years later he discovered the prayer wasn't even Hebrew, but Aramaic, an even more ancient language, and supposedly the one Jesus spoke. (He loved that.) And it was even more years later that he finally found a translation. And it didn't mention death once. So how could it be a prayer for the dead?

He knew his Hebrew school education would end as soon as he had his bar-mitzvah. His mother told him on more than one occasion that if he wanted to quit, once he'd done that deed, she'd have no problem with him leaving it forever. And just like the early battles he'd lost, he knew it was no use trying to fight having a bar-mitzvah. He was stuck, because of his age, and his inability to run away, which he knew he'd never do.

The one saving grace, in his mind, was one he never

voiced to anyone, his true revenge on these years of toil that were forced upon him. His true revenge on his father, who made him do something he'd always hated, from the first day, to the last.

Whenever the time came, no matter how old he was, he swore that he'd never say the Kaddish for his father, upon his death.

So when he finished his haftorah, stepping down from the bima, seeing the tears in the eyes of his grandparents, and especially in the eyes of his great-grandfather Max who had lived to see that momentous day, and the look of pride on the faces of his parents, he thought, as his father shook his hand for perhaps the only time in his life, as he looked into his father's proud eyes, he thought, no way, old man. I won't say it for you. You'll be trapped in your coffin forever, forever sealed in the earth, unable to break free from your physical bonds, stuck to your rotting skeleton because of what you made me do, taking five years of my young life to fix your own.

No way.

Of course, he didn't know then, so young and still basically innocent, how wrong he would be.

Worn Silk and Cracked Leather

Blake arrived at the synagogue early. Almost fifteen years had passed since he'd last been here. It hadn't changed, a stark structure of old brick with no adornments of any kind. In the cool morning air the sounds of his leather shoes were sharp on the stone steps. The sun was bright, the day brisk. He took a deep breath, barely invigorated by the cold rush that filled his lungs, and opened the heavy wooden door.

Exhaustion wrapped his body like an old blanket. Too many sleepless nights in a row, living on alcohol and cigarettes, which was not his usual style. He hardly drank a drop and never smoked. Yet this past week, as he drifted further from his family, those vices fit. Now his mouth tasted foul, a sticky film covered his teeth. He knew he needed a shave. He'd promised Jake and his wife Molly he would try this. And so he was here.

The air inside was stale; the lobby dark. Religion had always been a shroud of darkness to him, probably because of this place and the people he had encountered here. He remembered a constant absence of color, and of joy, except at holidays, when the release of pent-up emotion surged all around him. He was surprised at how tiny a building it was. In his memory it was a huge monolith of righteousness. Off to the left was the Rabbi's study, where they said the morning Kaddish. The door was shut, but he heard murmuring on the other side. He grabbed the tarnished brass doorknob, turned it slowly, and went in.

He would rather have been anywhere else this morning, even back at the cemetery, than here. He didn't want to do this, to say the Kaddish for his father, in a minyan. He'd sworn on more than one occasion this day would never come. But his mother had asked him. Her asking was more a begging. Her grief was palpable. She'd asked both her sons, but Jake had held firm, and simply said, No, Ma, it won't matter if I do or don't, so I won't. So when she held him by the shoulders, and begged him, he couldn't refuse her tears.

Scanning the room, he quickly counted. He was the ninth. Some of the old men looked at him, disinterested, went back to their quiet talking. Those rules hadn't changed. A quorum was still ten. Now he had to wait for someone else. He'd never understood the meaning of the numbers. Why couldn't it be nine? Wasn't nine a magic number? Ten seemed meaningless.

He barely remembered the prayer, had never known it completely. If the tenth man showed, it would be the same old scene he'd partaken in when young: all of them huddled and mumbling together the ancient prayer for the dead. Would he be able to read the words? Then again, there was no reason why he would have to say it aloud. None of these old men would. They'd all sway in their davening, practically hum the words, bending at the knees at the mention of the many names of God. He'd imitate them. He was great at faking this kind of thing. He had never paid attention when he was a student here, had learned only the beginnings of every prayer. Once things got going, and the congregation joined in, or when silent prayer was called for, Blake looked the part. The eight men present wore their prayer shawls, patiently waiting. If someone else didn't come soon, they'd break up, and Blake would have wasted the morning.

Blake hadn't brought his own tallis, since his father was buried in it. He thought of the mad rush he and Jake had made for the funeral parlor, six days ago. They had to bring a suit of his father's for him to be buried in, his army discharge papers for the flag, and his father's tallis. "Where's Daddy's tallis?" he'd screamed at his mother. She was in shock and seemed not to hear, sitting on the edge of the bed watching her sons tear the place apart. Finally he found his own, buried in a drawer. "Here's mine, c'mon, let's go." And then they'd gone shopping for their father's coffin.

The cardboard box was still by the door, full of "generic" tallises, for those like Blake who didn't have one. He grabbed a tattered one off the top, threw it around his shoulders. It was faded, stained, smelled vaguely of camphor. He took the yarmulke out of his pocket and stuck it on his head.

He sat down beside an ancient grizzled man with rheumy eyes. The old man had a horrible odor and tufts of hair growing out of his ears. These men were probably all retired. He imagined them spending their days in the synagogue, arguing over the Talmud, not doing any good to anyone. Some were obviously retired businessmen, talking the stock market. A few were members of the synagogue, who came every morning to say their prayers. And one or two were like the man Blake sat next to, poor religious fools who spent the day in the synagogue because it was warm and safe from the cruel world outside. He was supposed to come and say Kaddish for a month. He'd give it this one day. His mother would have to accept it.

A few of the men wore T'fillin, the phylacteries. He'd once owned a set of the small leather boxes, had even liked the novelty of strapping them to his forehead and arm, with the long strip of leather that wound around his head down his arm, ending around his fingers to delineate a Hebrew letter.

When he was twelve he and his friends had played with their T'fillin, swinging the boxes around their heads by the leather strips, singing "Holy boxes, holy boxes, we're not gonna eat our bagels and loxes," until his father had come upon them and screamed bloody murder. His father had thrown them out of the house. Why the hell did he care? He didn't give a damn about any religion. Why should he care that his son was misusing some holy artifact? He didn't even know what the boxes were for, couldn't even put them on. In his father's great plan to train his son in the religion he'd never known himself, he'd far surpassed his father in knowledge, but still profaned anything his father might have thought holy. But after that day he'd never played with the T'fillin again, and never strapped those boxes to his forehead, either. He had no idea where his T'fillin was now. Somewhere in his mother's attic, probably.

The pious few who were wearing them today were already lost in their morning prayers. Outside he heard children on their way to school. Their happy patter sounded as clean as the outside air, and he wanted to be with them. Their sounds caused him to think back to when he'd been a child, in the summer, playing as the night came on, feeling the cool air replace the warmth of the day. If he was sunburned he would feel a chill. He could almost hear his father's voice calling him, pulling him away from the fun.

"Dov? Is it Dov?"

The old man sitting next to him, the one with the stink and the hair in his ears, was talking to him. Dov? He hadn't heard that word since he'd been a student at this place so long ago.

"That's my Hebrew name. Do I know you?"

"Meyers. Rabbi Meyers. It's Dov, yes?"

Rabbi Meyers, the mean one, who'd on more than one occasion thrown him out of the building for his insolence and disrespect. Who called him no good and told him that he would never amount to anything. Who picked his nose in a tranced state and often fell asleep while the class read prayers out loud.

"Yes. Hello, Rabbi. I'm surprised you remember me."

"Ah, Dov. You I don't forget, even with the beard.

You gave me some trouble."

"Yes, I suppose I did."

"So tell me, Dov. You don't have a tallis? You wear an old one."

The rabbi touched the tallis, fingering the torn cloth. Blake wanted to pull away, tell him to get his filthy hands off him. Nobody had touched him since the funeral. He wouldn't let his wife near him. Molly had kept her distance, thinking that was what he needed. He didn't want to talk to this old rabbi. He didn't want to be touched by him. He wanted to be back home, mourning with his family. He wanted a drink.

"I had one, Rabbi," he said, tugging the tallis out of the old man's hands. "My father is buried in it."

"Ah," Rabbi Meyers said, a crooked sad smile on his face, "my condolences. But T'fillin," he pointed with his head to the men who wore them, "you know T'fillin?"

Where was the tenth man, so they could start this charade? How long could he endure this pathetic remnant of his past?

"You had T'fillin. I taught you, no?"

"Yes. I don't know where it is."

A tenth man walked in. A minyan. Thank God. Now it could start. The tenth man found his place. The others who had not done so opened their prayer books and began. Rabbi Meyers motioned to the tenth man, and they walked to the corner of the study, whispering, looking at Blake. They were obviously friends. He tried to ignore them. He opened his prayer book, found the place, but Rabbi Meyers came over, pointing with an arthritic finger. The tenth man had gone out but was back. A few of the other ancients looked over approvingly while they prayed.

The tenth man gave Meyers a worn felt bag. He watched as the rabbi unzipped it and took out a very old set of T'fillin. The leather was cracked with age, the little boxes warped. Rabbi Meyers unfurled the long leather straps and reached out to Blake, who glanced into the small mirror next to the bookshelves, caught his reflection, stared at his face, his eyes puffed from too much whiskey and crying. He flinched, pulled back, almost dropped his prayer book.

A scene flashed into his mind from his childhood. Meyers had humiliated him. The class had been studying the Passover seder service. He'd made some crack in his usual style, and the Rabbi had exploded. Meyers had grabbed him by the neck and thrown him out of the room. Blake still clutched the Passover Haggadah. He opened the door, came back into the classroom, and screaming curses at the Rabbi, threw the Haggadah against the wall. It fell to the ground. The class came to a hushed silence. Meyers ran to the wall, picked it up, kissed its covers. It was the first time he'd ever seen tears in a grown man's eyes. The Rabbi tried to speak, looked to the class, opened his mouth. No sound came out. He turned back to Blake, who stood paralyzed, unable to move. Then Blake ran out of the room. He ended up in his secret place behind the synagogue, where he went sometimes to be alone, and cried for hours.

He'd never wanted to attend Hebrew school. His father wanted Blake to go, he'd known this his whole life, not so he would learn something of importance that was being passed from one generation to another, not so he would enter some unknown spiritual world his father loved so much and wanted to share. No, he knew his father wanted only one thing: that upon his death his son would say Kaddish for him, to assure his everlasting peace.

He'd tried every tactic he'd ever learned in the subtle family manipulations that had in the past gotten him what he wanted, but what kind of power does an eight year old have against his father? So he went, hating every minute he was forced to go, and his father seemed satisfied.

At every religious occasion, Blake mocked the rituals, and resented the fact that his father was so obviously proud of Blake's accomplishments, and now he could acknowledge these were the only times he'd ever seen anything resembling pride coming from his father. But there were rare occasions when Blake was able to step outside of this anger and be genuinely awed by the mysteries of religion, the hugeness of this God that was unnameable, with a face that would blind anyone who tried to look upon it. He struggled against this attraction, and instead caused havoc in the Hebrew school, causing Rabbi Meyers more trouble than he was worth. Blake thought, years later, that he'd needed some guidance in religion, from someone who saw in the depths of the mysteries what he himself thought might be there. But Meyers was devoid of any deeper knowledge, he understood even as a child. The old rabbi only went through the motions because those were the rules. When he was finally bar-mitzvah, and officially graduated from the place, he swore he'd never return, never say a Kaddish for his father. It was an unspoken rift between them that never healed, and Blake felt as if it was the one triumph he had over the old man.

Yet here he was, hungover and confused. Why had he come? Just to please his mother? Because Jake had refused so stubbornly? What was he trying to prove? He'd always believed that his father had kept him away from whatever joy and comfort he might have found in his religion, in effect sending him into exile. But in mourning, he wondered if that was a lie. He'd kept himself away from his heritage. The only one he could save was himself. But could he? Who was he trying to make peace with: himself? His father? God?

Now Blake felt like he was being manhandled by a giant insect. The rabbi's long cold fingers wrapped the leather around his arm. Blake remembered when he had been shown this in preparation for his bar-mitzvah. He'd hated the old man handling him, teaching him the ritual. Meyers had held him still with a steel grip and said through clenched teeth, "All my boys who are bar-mitzvah will know T'fillin. Even you, Dov." Now the Rabbi smiled his crooked sad smile, patted Blake's stubbled face as if he were a child again. A few of the men glanced over, pulled out of their prayers, and nodded.

"Now," the rabbi whispered, "say Kaddish for your father. He is with God now."

He tried to say the words, but he got lost as he knew would happen, and quietly changed to a monosyllabic nonsense, bowing when others bowed. He closed his eyes, then opened them again, coming back to his reflection, to see what he looked like, to see what he looked like praying. Old phylacteries and a borrowed tallis. He barely recognized himself.

He still felt the rabbi's fingers on his arms, on his face. He wanted to run out of there and tear the leather off, throw it into the sky. He was strangling, the leather felt like a noose, a straitjacket. The little box stuck to his forehead weighed him down, burned into his skin. He didn't know how long it would last, but he would stand until the last one stood. He davened like the best of them, mumbling sounds and occasionally raising his voice and he lost himself to the green walls, to the cries of the children outside, and to the memories of summers past.

He felt the walls closing in around him and stared at the drunken eyes in the reflection. He saw in his bloodshot eyes these past days when he had paced the hospital floor, waiting, out of breath from running from the airport. He and his family were led into the ICU, and he had watched his father, bloated with drugs, hooked up to machines, falter, fade, and finally die. He saw himself that night informing his relatives, one drunken phone call following another, Jake gently taking the phone from him, whispering, "Blake, I'll do that, you go and lie down." And he saw in the reflection the days of mourning after he had buried his father, who'd died too soon and too suddenly. He saw the drinking which dulled the pain and the anger he felt because he wasn't ready for all of this. He saw the sleepless nights and wasted, stinking days.

And he felt the mysteries all around him, even if these old forgotten men had no idea what they were immersed in. This ancient incantation, this prayer for the dead. There was a power in this prayer, and even though he was far away from the actual meaning of the words, he knew. Maybe his father had known too, maybe not, but he understood now that his father always had the fear. The old man's biggest fear was that he'd die with no one to say these holy words for him, that he'd die and face God with nothing to show but an empty life, to be ultimately forgotten back on earth.

Blake struggled to find his place in the prayer book, to offer his father something the old man had needed so badly that he'd sacrificed his oldest son on the altar of this knowledge. Blake saw himself in the reflection of the mirror and the T'fillin now looked to him like a huge bandage covering his arm, his neck, his whole head, and he saw the wounds exposed to the air underneath, he could almost see the blood, and he swayed, lowering at the knees and upright again, always coming back to his reflection, and filling up inside until, finally, here, standing among strange old men, covered in worn silk and cracked leather, singing a prayer for the dead in an alien language, he thought he would burst.

Gdanke

She would always be Gdanke. She hated that she had a new name, Jennie. Who was Jennie? She had no idea. It happened on Ellis Island. Her brother, Moshe, she would also only ever think of as Moshe, not the name he gave himself, Julius. Sam, somehow, was an easy change for her. He would always be Sam (she pronounced his name "Sem"). Samuel and Shmuel, not much of a difference. But when she talked with Moshe, after they settled in Brooklyn, he would interrupt her and say, "Please, Jennie. I'm Julius now." And she would often say with anger, "And I am still Gdanke, Moshe!"

All she recalled from the journey over was a muddled collage of images. She was a small girl, and her main memory was fear. And darkness. And her mother's arms surrounding her, never letting her go. The mixture of languages was a dull sound that contained no words. Now and then her father would disappear, often taking

Moshe. They would go upstairs, they would go deeper into steerage. Being with just her mother and Shmuel gave her an even stronger fear, because she thought something would happen, what she had no idea, and then it would just be the three of them, alone.

But her father always returned. Once he had bread. He didn't say where or how he got it, but it was a welcome relief from the hardness of her mother's biscuits.

Rather than days in a row, a journey on the ocean to a new land and a new life, for Gdanke it was one long endless horrid uninterrupted day, where sleep and wakefulness were indistinguishable, where her dreams and the reality surrounding her had no boundaries, where there was no conversation, where she no longer recognized her parents' faces as those she knew back home, their expressions as if made of stone: grim, afraid, ungiving.

And then that long day ended, and she was taken from the bowels of the ship up into the air, and the resulting chaos was too much for her to understand. She held her mother's hand with all her strength. They followed her father and brothers, and before she knew it her father lifted her up and placed her on a huge crate, telling her to sit there and not move.

The crate. Another boat. Shoving crowds. A city in the distance. Long lines. And her brother Moshe in charge, leading them, talking with officials. More lines. Incredibly loud echoing roars of thousands of people in huge rooms. Babies crying. Children screaming. Yelling. Laughter. Anger.

It seemed she left one nightmare for another.

And then a shorter line. A smaller room. The roaring crowds receded. And her brother saying words she didn't quite understand.

"Max," he said, pointing to his father, "Dorothy," pointing to his mother, and then, pointing to her and her brother, "Jennie, Sam."

Onto another boat, her father and brother dragging that huge crate that appeared out of thin air, and then the last part of the journey, her exhaustion making it hard to stand, hard to walk, even hard to breathe. She had no idea how much time passed, but at some point they stood on the steps of a house, her father knocking on the door, a man she didn't know opening it, her father and the man embracing, and then they were inside the house where she saw a couch. She was on it and asleep in seconds.

When she opened her eyes she was in a bed, and her mother, her real actual mother, sat beside her, watching her awaken. Her mother smiled, stroked her cheek.

"Ah," her mother said, smiling, "my baby awakes!"

Her brother Moshe entered the room and saw her with eyes opened, and his face beamed.

"There you are!" he cried. "Our Jennie, back from the dead!"

She didn't know what he meant.

"Gdanke," she said, thinking he'd forgotten her name.

"We are in a new country," he said gently, "and so we must have new names. Your brother Moshe? I am now Julius!" He laughed. "Yes! And Mama is Dorothy. And you are Jennie! American names!"

She looked at her mother for rescue from this nonsense. Her mother shook her head.

"Your brother," she said, "let him be. Come now, and we'll have some real food. Soup!"

At home, once they had their home, she was sometimes Jennie, sometimes Gdanke. Her brother now seemed to be the head of the family. He found a school, and brought her there to be enrolled. Her brother knew English, and it seemed that was the way to get things done. She stood beside him, heard him say, "Jennie Rosen," and before she knew it he left her there in a room full of children her age, who eyed her with distrust.

She eventually got used to going, slowly learned enough English to make her way, but the work was hard, and her mornings almost always started with her in trouble, as attendance was called. When her teacher called out, "Jennie Rosen," she rarely responded, because she never heard her name. One time she was drawing circles on some paper when she realized the teacher was standing next to her. She looked up.

"Are you here today, Jennie Rosen?" the teacher, an old woman with her hair in a tight bun and small glasses on her nose, said.

"Gdanke," she replied.

"Not in my classroom," the teacher said, "in here you are Jennie Rosen. Gdanke is the girl who came here, but she is no more. Do you understand?"

She nodded, but thought, *I understand that you are wrong.*

She made few friends, but worked hard to follow

the lessons. Her English improved, and though she still spoke Yiddish at home with her parents, she tried to teach them what she learned. Helping her mother cook, she would always hold up an ingredient before it got chopped, or peeled, or put in soup or dough or in the oven, and say its name for her mother in Yiddish, and then say it again, in English.

Time passed. School became a routine. Her parents joined a small synagogue that was somehow connected to their synagogue back in Budapest. They lit Shabbos candles on Friday nights. Her brother Moshe got a job. Sam was sometimes in school, sometimes on the streets with his new friends. She tried hard to remember her old life, and would often go to sleep thinking of their house, her father's stall in the market, her grandparents, but in time, as Brooklyn became more and more familiar, her other life became hazy and indistinct. She'd sometimes cry herself to sleep, wishing they'd never left.

But life did not stop. More time passed. She made challahs with her mother for Friday night dinners. Her father now worked in a shoe store in the neighborhood. Moshe now seemed like a man. Sam, she realized, had started shaving. She knew that, had they still lived in Budapest, he would be growing a beard.

One night, as her mother watched her braid the challah, she said, "Mama, will I ever marry?"

"What do you mean?" her mother said. "Of course you will marry!"

"But there are no matchmakers here in Brooklyn."

"Well, no, but our synagogue is how a match will

take place. My beautiful girl, you will make some lucky man a wonderful wife! Now, the poppy seeds."

And that ended the discussion.

She knew that the crate her father had found on the boat was filled with treasure. She rarely saw the insides. That one time they opened it upon their arrival in Brooklyn was a dim memory; she had been so exhausted she barely knew what was happening. It sat in one room covered with a linen sheet. Her brother Sam told her one time, in a whisper, that it was a gift from God. It helped her father feed the family. It helped get them their tenement apartment. Whatever hardships came their way, what was inside that crate would get them through it.

Her English improved, even her accent became less blunt and obvious. She finished ninth grade and her father said that she didn't need to do any more school. So she found a job in a small market in the neighborhood that reminded her of home. The owner was a member of their synagogue, and she liked going there, talking with the people who came in, many of whom she knew from the services. The seasons came and went, marked by Jewish holidays that were familiar and warm. Her routines of work, home, cooking with her mother, the occasional holiday service, gave her life a comforting pattern.

And then her life unraveled in a way she could never have predicted. It started with her brother Moshe, who announced one night that he was going to give back to his new country: he was going to enlist in the Armed Forces. Their father argued against this; for him, military service meant joining a group that was no place for Jews.

Julius (still Moshe in her mind) argued one night at the dinner table that, although this was true back where they came from, now it meant freedom and the ability to choose.

"I forbid this!" her father said, slamming his hand on the table.

She jumped.

But rather than matching her fear, her brother laughed. She and Sam looked at each other, ready for an argument that would shake the roof.

"Father," Moshe said, "I am eighteen! Not only have I been bar-mitzvah, which means I'm a man as far as Jews go, I'm also a man as far as America goes."

"You are still my son," her father said.

"Yes, and I will always be your son. But dear father, you cannot dictate what I can and cannot do. Not now. Not here."

He winked at Gdanke.

"Not ever, eh Jennie?"

"If father cannot make you stay at home, because of this freedom," she said, "then I can take this name, Jennie, and I can toss it out the window!"

Moshe laughed again, loud and full of love.

"You will always be my beautiful sister," he said, tearing challah from the loaf, filling his mouth with the warm bread, "and I don't care if you think of yourself as Charlie Chaplin! Ha!"

That was the beginning of the end, for Gdanke. Her brother came home one day in his new uniform, and marched around the apartment like a little boy who'd found a new toy. He was to report to basic training far away, in Kansas, in two weeks, first stopping at an Army Training Center in New Jersey. Their parents were petrified of him leaving, even though he'd tried to make them feel secure knowing that Sam was a responsible replacement for him, as far as dealing with anything outside the home. And, Sam would be put in charge of the treasure in the crate masquerading as a table. But they didn't want him going alone. There didn't seem to be a solution, but one night, Sam came up with an idea.

"Why doesn't Gdanke go with him?" he said.

This seemed even more idiotic than him going alone.

"Sam," she said, "why are you talking such nonsense?"

Even Moshe thought it was ridiculous.

"And then she comes back home, alone? On a train? From Kansas?" he said.

But Sam said, no, not at all. First, Gdanke would accompany Julius only to New Jersey. Once he was at the Army Training Center, they'd be in charge of him. And, Gdanke wouldn't return alone. They would go with another: their cousin David, the son of the first cousin they met when they came to Brooklyn those years ago. David, then, was a shy boy who Gdanke barely registered as living in the same house. But she got to know him over the years, and they would sit next to each other at family seders. She liked David. And she wanted to accompany her brother on the beginning of his journey. The trip would also give her more time with him.

So that was the decision, and she looked forward to this with an excitement she never allowed herself on her last journey, the trip over with her family. That voyage, for her, was only fear and the unknown. This time, she'd be with her brother and cousin, and they wouldn't travel far, at least not as far as Moshe.

She barely had time to register that this would mean Moshe would be gone from their lives, when the time came for them to leave.

The second way in which her life continued to unravel was connected to the trip, but not caused by it. She'd heard her parents talking one night about something happening in Brooklyn. Her father said there was a sickness. He'd read of it in the Forward, the Yiddish paper he brought home every night. People were dying. Whatever it was, was spreading.

"Who is dying?" her mother said.

"People!" her father said.

"I don't know anyone with such a sickness."

And neither did she. She continued to work at the market, right up until the day they were to catch the train to Manhattan. The day before they were to depart, her cousin David came over to make sure she was ready. He said he had something to show her, and proceeded to open a small box he'd carried into the house. Gdanke saw a small black flat rectangle and had no idea what this was.

"Watch this," he said, and the rectangle opened up, unfolded, and he held it up as if he'd just done a magic trick. "Voila!"

"David," she said, "what is this thing?"

"This, dear cousin, is how we will record our journey with Julius. This is a camera."

She was unimpressed, even though she'd never seen one before.

She hadn't handled her small bag since she'd lugged it from Budapest all those years ago, so when she unsnapped the small latches and opened it, she could have sworn she smelled home, their real home. This time, though, she didn't have to pack it so tightly with everything from her former life. She filled it with some clothes, her hair brush and toothbrush, and a periodical she liked to read, *The American Magazine*, that was filled with stories by American writers. She and David were going to spend one night in New Jersey at the home of cousins of David's from the side of his family she didn't know. She'd never spent a night away from her parents, and thought, with her magazine, she'd be occupied with fiction, to calm her nervousness, which wouldn't abate.

Even though she would be with David and Moshe, she wished Sam was going instead. But Sam insisted she go. She knew that for Sam, her and Moshe going meant some time for him to be on his own.

Her last dinner with both her brothers and her parents, was uneventful, even though she was hardly able to eat her mother's wonderful food. She wanted to say something, to acknowledge her trepidation, but whatever she said fell on deaf ears.

"Do you think I'll enjoy this trip?" she said.

"What's to enjoy?" her father said. "You are taking Julius to the army. In New Jersey. David is going to bring you back. This is not an enjoying trip. It's not even a trip. It's two days."

"Mama," she said, giving it one more try, "can't Sam go?"

"No," her mother said, "Sam is needed here if Moshe goes away."

She knew there was no winning this argument, so after cleaning the kitchen, she went directly to her bed. Sleeping would be better than being awake, thinking of what lay ahead.

She felt a slight chill getting into her bed, and when she woke the next morning, her nose was running. This was something she did not need, to catch a cold on the first day of the journey. She thought of saying to her mother, how can I go? I'm getting sick! But knew a cold would not be enough to keep her home. Her excitement mixed with her nervousness, and she decided, this will be – this has to be – a journey of fun. Cold or no cold. Two days or twenty days.

David arrived when he said he would, and she and Moshe and David kissed her parents, and Sam, goodbye, and made their way to the train, to get the ferry in Manhattan that would bring Moshe to his first training camp in New Jersey.

Her last life-changing journey, she was a young girl driven to exhaustion, and her memories were few. This time she was determined to think of it only as an adventure, in spite of her anxiety. She wanted to remember everything. She continuously asked her cousin to take pictures: as they boarded the train in Brooklyn, as they boarded the ferry to cross the Hudson, and as her cold slowly became more of a nuisance.

Gdanke had only ever taken the train that one day

when her family arrived at Ellis Island. The IRT line went over the Brooklyn Bridge, and she'd never experienced anything like it. This time was no less exciting. The trip wasn't long, but she was aware of being high above the water on this bridge. In the distance she saw the Statue of Liberty, and vaguely recalled seeing it on the day their journey to America ended. She didn't quite understand why there was a green lady holding a torch that seemed to be rising from the water, but now, looking out at Liberty Island, she thought, she's welcoming us. She welcomed us on that horrible day those years ago. I didn't see it then. I see it now.

Her cold seemed to get worse by the minute, and when they boarded the ferry to Jersey, her head was pounding. But she refused to let this trifle ruin their trip together. She felt protective of Moshe, even though it was clear, watching him sitting there, his excitement, his innocence, that he didn't really need her, or their cousin. He was off on an adventure that would take him far away, and his experiences would be his own. She and David were only a small part of the beginning.

Seeing him so full of wonder, as he watched the world from the train on this bridge, in his new uniform, his face clean-shaven, his eyes wide, she couldn't help but think, that's Julius. Not Moshe.

My brother, Julius, the American.

Not Exactly

It wasn't until Blake was home for his grandmother's funeral that he tried to squeeze the truth out of his mother about the crystal. He felt like he'd gotten pretty much all he could from his grandmother, his Uncle Sam, and his parents about the mysterious Uncle Julius, who in the words of his great-uncle, 'saved the family.' How this occurred, or what it even was, still remained unanswered.

His grandfather had died the previous year, and he'd returned from college for the funeral. Unlike the ambivalence he felt towards things like Jewish rituals, and the Kaddish in particular, he gladly stood with his father and Jake at the cemetery, intoning those ancient words for his grandfather, who he adored.

When he was young, his grandfather would often arrive on Sunday, when the family had no plans to visit cousins or either set of grandparents. His grandfather always said he was going to check on the laundry, and would the boys like to come along? The brothers knew that although the laundry would be the ultimate destination, their Gramps would first take them to the place that seemed so foreign even though they knew it was still Brooklyn.

Coney Island.

They never did much there. Steeplechase was long gone, although the huge sign remained. He wondered what it was all about, but just seeing that giant clown-like painting of the smiling man, high above the chaos of noise and people below, made him realize there was a whole world that used to exist here. The parachute ride was also closed, but the poetic skeleton of that contraption still rose higher than any building to be seen. The old Cyclone still rumbled on its wooden tracks, but he had no desire to risk his life on such a thing.

So they'd walk around, people watch, and their grandfather would usually bring them to Nathan's for the best French fries he'd ever had. When he got a little older, there'd be a hamburger as well, dripping with grease and fried onions. Jake often got cotton candy after his fries, but Blake liked the soggy burgers.

Then they'd go to the carousel. Gramps would buy them tickets, usually for just one ride, but on the rare special Sunday, they'd ride twice. Blake always imagined he was on a real horse – he had a rocking horse at home where he'd zone out for hours, in a repetitive meditative motion of up and back, up and back – and at the carousel he often rode the same horse, imagining himself off on some adventure, riding at a full gallop, the wind in his face, the sounds of the horse's hooves filling him with glee.

Blake is convinced that the reason he ended up living out west, at least partly, is because he wanted to ride real horses in real mountains, and have what he could only imagine as a child.

After the carousel, they'd return to the car, and their Gramps would take them to the laundry, where first he'd head to the Coke machine, take out a key and open it, and give them each bottles of liquid caffeine. He'd run his finger around the bottles' tops, once he uncapped them, to make sure there were no jagged edges or chips of glass. He'd hand them each one, and leave them to their guzzling.

Then he'd go up the narrow stone stairs to the office, while they caroused around the whole place, taking turns in the huge laundry carts, while the other pushed it around, knocking into walls, crashing into tables, whooping it up completely buzzed on the soda they'd never be permitted at home. When they were allowed soda at home, which wasn't often – milk was the drink their mother gave them at meals – it was only orange soda. Which had its own great sugar rush, but Coke was a whole other buzz.

Blake never knew what his grandfather did up there in the office, but he'd eventually come down, call out their names, and back in the car they'd go to be brought home, where they'd crash from the comedown of greasy foods, the sugar, and the caffeine.

His grandmother didn't recover well from the death of her husband, but Blake was still not ready to hear that his mother's mother had died barely a year after her father. He was out of college, still living upstate, working in a bookstore, and basically living his college life with the same friends who stayed in town, most of them starting their post-college lives, a few off to other cities for grad school, med school, or moving back to the city to live with their parents until they made their true move into their lives.

He flew home, and it was a somber affair. At the cemetery he couldn't take his eyes off his grandfather's gravestone, staring at the name, with a birth date and a date of death. And the blank space below his grandfather's name, he understood, would soon be chiseled in.

After the graveside service, they returned to his grandparents' house, where he'd spent so many days playing with the old photos in the small cabinet on Sunday visits, where they'd had countless Passover Seders, break-the-fasts after Yom Kippur, Thanksgivings, where he'd hang with his cousins, and where time seemed to stand still, at least for a while.

The house seemed more than empty, even though it was filled with all his relatives, and some friends of his grandparents that he didn't know. His Great-Aunt-Rose sat in the corner, on an old armchair, and she seemed lost, her orange wig a bit askew, her rosy cheeks a bit too bright. He watched as his Uncle Sam brought her a cup of coffee. Her hands shook as she took it. He stood beside her, in a protective way, while she sipped.

He wasn't in any sort of mood to answer questions from his elders. Still upstate? How was college? Any plans? Grad school? Girlfriend? So he walked alone around the house, staring at the family pictures on the walls, avoiding any kind of interaction. He did spend a bit of time in the backyard with some of his cousins, and one of them pulled out a joint, which he lit before Blake could try and stop it, and it got passed among the younger generation, and once he was stoned, he was glad his cousin brought it. They just hung together, mostly in silence, all mildly stoned, while the afternoon waned and the light faded.

Much later, after almost everyone had gone, after his mother and aunt had cleaned up, his mother was on the couch, seemingly lost in thought. His father was in the kitchen with his aunt and uncle, so he went and sat next to his mother to see if he could cheer her up. He had no idea where Jake had gone.

She took his hand and they sat together in silence. He knew he should say something, but 'Sorry for your loss,' did not seem appropriate.

"They had good lives," she finally said to him.

"What'll happen to the house?" he said.

"We'll sell it, and probably sell most of the furniture. Nana had a few photo albums that I'll take, unless my sister wants them."

"You mean all those pictures that used to be in the bottom of the cabinet?"

"I'm sure," she said, "and probably more. I think she had pictures stashed everywhere."

Blake had no idea then that eventually he'd inherit all those albums, and spend a whole summer putting them in chronological order, and rediscover the photo of his Uncle Julius.

"What about the crystal? You won't sell that?"

There were still a few pieces from the ancient crystal he and Jake had played with as boys, now prominently displayed around the house, no longer in danger from small children with grabby hands.

"No," she said. "We'll probably share that among all you kids. There isn't much left from what there was when I was a girl."

He hadn't planned on grilling his mother about the crystal, but now that they'd started, he thought, *here's my chance to learn something.*

"How much more was there?"

He could see her going back to her own childhood, by the way she looked off into some familiar distance.

"It was something," she said. "There was a huge wooden crate when I was little, in the basement, where the washing machine is now. I used to climb up onto it and pretend I was on a stage. Your aunt and I would put on plays for each other. That crate used to be full of the most beautiful crystal. Plates, wine glasses, bowls, decanters, so much more. My mother would open it and use it for the huge Passover seders she had in the 30's and 40's, when I grew up. We called it the Family Circle. A whole extended family, most now gone, many I no longer even know where they are now, many right off the boat, would all be welcome. Sometimes there would be over thirty people. My mother did all the cooking – she'd start two weeks ahead, buy flats of eggs, dozens of eggs, she'd have live pike in the bathtub for the gefilte fish. That seems a long, long time ago."

He'd never heard of such a thing, a family circle. It reminded him for a second of the way he'd think of Coney Island when his grandfather took him and Jake there; a lost world.

"Wait," he said, "a wooden crate? Full of crystal? I thought Grandpa found the crystal in a hole in the wall in the office of the laundry. Right?"

She stroked his hand and looked at him as if he was a child again.

"Well," she said, with a soft chuckle, "not exactly."

He waited for her to say more, but then she was once again lost in thought. This could be his only chance.

"Okay," he said, "okay, then, what? Exactly?"

He thought for a second she was going to get up and leave him without answers. She stirred, but he held her hand, she settled in, and took a deep breath.

"There was a lot more when I was a kid," she said. "There was a hole in the wall in the laundry, but that's not where my father found it. That's where he hid it. Or hid some of it."

"Hid it? From who?"

"I don't know if my Uncle Sam would want me to be telling you all this."

Just as she said this, he saw Sam helping Rose into her coat, and his father, aunt and uncle, all said, bye! See you tomorrow!

He waved to his mother and Blake over on the couch, and then they were out the door.

"Why not?" he said, frustrated that he wouldn't have the chance to grill his great-uncle.

"It's not really my business. And I don't know much. My mother knew a lot, and well, tomorrow we start sitting shiva for her. Uncle Sam will be here. You can ask him then, and I'm sure he'll tell you whatever you want to know."

Shiva

Although Jake offered Blake a place to stay while he was in town for their grandmother's funeral, he'd decided to stay with his parents, and sleep in his own bed. He figured he'd get up, have breakfast with his folks, then they'd drive over to his grandmother's house together, to begin the official sitting of shiva, the week-long Jewish ritual meant as a memorial for the deceased.

But when Blake got up, the house seemed too quiet, and he knew he was alone. His parents had left without him. There was a note on the kitchen table, "Jake will pick you up," so he got himself dressed, made himself a cup of coffee, and waited for his brother to show.

Jake didn't come in, but honked his horn with two quick beeps. Blake was out and in the car before he had to honk again.

"Ready Jakie?" he said, strapping in.

"Who's ever ready for shiva, huh?"

Blake had only been to a few shivas in his life, for both his grandfathers, now both his grandmothers, and the parent of an old friend, when they were in high school. He always thought it was a strange gathering, and never felt ready for, or used to, this important rite for any Jewish family; the immediate family sitting on small cardboard boxes instead of chairs, too much food and liquor, and, strangest of all, every mirror in the house covered with a sheet.

For his friend's dad, he remembered staying in his friend's room, the two of them sitting together on the bed, not talking about the fact that they'd just been to the funeral of his friend's dad. But he was glad he was there. His friend needed him, so they sat in silence for hours with the radio on.

At the shiva for his father's father, he'd not been there long, and was given permission to head home after an hour or so. When his father's mother died, he'd wanted to stay around, because his cousins were all there and they were able to be together in the basement while the adults did their visiting upstairs, so although he officially was at a shiva, he felt removed from the actual thing.

For his mother's father, he participated more, seeing a bit of why the ritual was important. It was obvious to him, then, that people needed a way to connect without ignoring the sadness of the death of their loved one. So he let himself be part of a few conversations, and enjoyed the laughter when it happened, a soothing balm that covered everyone.

"A lot of people there yesterday," Jake said, parking down the street from his grandparents' house.

"My guess is it'll be crowded today too, but I hope to sit with Uncle Sam, get him talking."

"Talking?"

"Mom said something yesterday. Remember that crystal there was so much of, when we were kids?"

"How could I forget? I killed dragons with that long pointy thing."

"There was a lot of it."

"I still have a dish, I use it for my keys and spare change."

"Where'd it come from, you remember the story, Jake?"

"Of course. Grandpa found it in the wall of the laundry office."

"Mom said he didn't find it, but he hid it there."

"No way. Truth? Hid it from who?"

"She said I should ask Uncle Sam."

There was a small group standing outside, mingling, chatting, as they approached the house. Blake scanned the group but didn't see either of his parents, or Uncle Sam. The brothers walked through the small crowd, as people stopped them for hugs, pats on the shoulder, kisses on the cheek. They knew they were required to be inside, so they walked up the steps and went to join the actual shiva.

There were more people inside than out. He was surprised there were so many. Both the kitchen and dining room tables were packed with food. Where he would normally have seen his grandmother in charge of everything, ruling the event from the kitchen, instead was his great Aunt Rose, obviously in charge. She saw him and waved him over.

"Blake," she said, kissing him, "go sit with your mother and aunt and Sam. They've been waiting for you." Her normally askew wig was neatly coiffed, and seeing her wearing his grandmother's apron made him do a double take.

"Okay," he said, as she literally turned him around and pushed him out of the kitchen.

It was strange seeing his mother and aunt sitting on those little cardboard boxes. Where did they get these things? Where do you buy a cardboard box for shiva? At the synagogue? The funeral home? This time he'd finally ask. His mother sat next to his aunt, Sam sat on a third, and there was a fourth box next to Sam, waiting.

He was here today to offer comfort to his mother, and his aunt, help where he could, being some kind of strength, hopefully, with his presence. It was weird seeing his father in the kitchen, helping Aunt Rose. She ordered his father and uncle both, handing them plates, having them clear empty dishes, obviously enjoying the role. He understood that the two men, along with Rose, were shielding their wives from any kitchen work that needed to be done as more people came, many who were at the funeral the day before.

It was a noisy pandemonium, and sounded more like a party than a memorial. Which, he thought, approaching his mother, aunt, and Sam, is what shiva really was. It wasn't supposed to be sad. The first day was always crowded. With each passing day, fewer and fewer would come to pay their respects. By the end of the week, he knew, it would be his parents, Jake, his aunt and uncle, and Uncle Sam and Aunt

Rose.

Today, though, Blake had an actual agenda, and didn't want to just observe, as he'd done before, or even be part of conversations that usually had the deceased as a main character, as memories were relived, old family stories retold. Sam patted the box next to him, without getting up, so Blake sat right down. It was the first time he'd ever sat on one. The boxes were for the immediate, nuclear family, spouse, siblings, and children of the deceased. But Sam wanted Blake next to him, so he plopped down on a cubicle of cardboard.

Sam put his hand on Blake's knee, and squeezed.

"How you doing, Blake?" Sam said in his thick Brooklynese.

"I'm good, Uncle Sam. You?"

Sam shook his head, ran his hand over his baldness.

"Me. I'm the last one, Blake. With my sister gone, your Nana, I'm the only one left."

Jake came over with a glass of something obviously alcoholic, and handed it to Blake.

"Aunt Rose said I should give you this," he said. "A little early for schnapps!" He laughed. "How about that, I'm being bossed around by Aunt Rose!" And then he was back in the kitchen, taking orders.

Blake took a sip and winced. It surely was too early. But what the hell, bottoms up!

Sam pointed with his chin to the kitchen.

"Look at her, my Rose," he said, "finally the boss."

He shook his head.

"My sister never liked my Rose," he said.

"What? Oh, sure she did," Blake said, lying.

"No," Sam said, patting Blake on the knee, "in fact, I think she hated her."

"No," Blake said, beginning a protest.

"She hated that I married a dancer, she hated that Rose wore too much make-up, she hated that we never had kids."

"Aunt Rose was a dancer?"

Sam laughed.

"And look at her now, running my sister's shiva! Wearing her apron! Giving orders. Hah!"

"What was that about Aunt Rose was a dancer?" He didn't care about the crystal right then, he had to hear this.

"What, your mother never mentioned this? She used to love it when Rose and I came over when she was little. Rose would let her try on her earrings, which were always clip-ons, she would never have a needle making holes in her lobes, I'll tell you that. Yeah, she was what we called a flapper. She wore long strings of fake pearls and when she did her thing, they'd fly around her in these huge circles. She worked in one of those illegal drinking clubs during Prohibition. She was a waitress, a dancer, a hostess." He gave Blake a sidelong glance. "A beauty."

Sam reached over, took Blake's drink, took a huge slug, and held onto the glass. He looked over to the kitchen, and caught Jake's eye, waved him over.

"What can I get you, Uncle Sam?" Jake said, a towel draping his shoulder.

"Not me. Your brother. Bring him an orange juice. And here," he said, downing the last of the bourbon, handing the glass to Jake, "fill this one up again, won'tcha, Jakie?"

Jake gave Blake a look, eyebrows raised, but Blake shrugged, like, we don't give permission for Uncle Sam to have a drink.

"Yeah," Sam said. "I married a woman who would never satisfy my sister. But what did I care? Love is love. When it hits you, Blake, y'know, it hits."

Jake was back with two glasses.

"OJ for the kid," he said, giving Sam a wink, "and a grown-up drink for the grown up."

"Jakie!" Rose called from the kitchen, "get this garbage out already!"

"Gotta go," Jake said, laughing.

Sam sipped his drink this time, smacked his lips.

"Rose would never let me drink this early," he said. "But it's shiva, right? Drown our sorrows."

Blake sipped his orange juice, and did feel like a kid sitting next to his old great uncle.

"And this is my second shiva this month," Sam said, shaking his head.

"Your second? Who died?"

Blake could see Sam's eyes welling up. He took a long sip, worked the alcohol around in his mouth, swallowed, looked at Blake.

"My best friend in the world," Sam said. "I don't know if you ever met him. Maybe when you were small, at a seder, I don't know. Georgie Steffens. From the old neighborhood."

"Uncle Sam, I'm so sorry," Blake said, putting his hand on the old man's shoulder.

Sam shrugged.

"So I'm really the last, last in my family, last in my old neighborhood gang. Last one standing. Or sitting," he said, raising his glass, taking a sip.

"Were you still in touch?" Blake said.

"You know how it is," Sam said. "You get old, you slow down, you don't do much. We'd see each other here and there, usually at a luncheonette we'd been going to forever. Have a coffee, a danish, catch up. But he was a special guy. A tough kid, you know? I used to think Georgie would end up in prison somewhere. He got involved in some bad stuff when we were young."

"Bad stuff?"

Sam sipped his drink.

"My friend Georgie," he said, "he wasn't an immigrant, like me. He was born right here in Brooklyn. Only ever knew English. I had to learn, y'know, for me to go to school. He took me to Coney Island, first time I ever went. Boy that was a day I don't ever forget." Sam shook his head, took a sip, and looked into his glass.

"Look at that, empty again. Jake!" he called, "get over here!"

Jake came over, took his brother's and uncle's glasses.

"Yes sir," he said, "more of the same?"

"I'll have what he's having," Blake said, "I think I'll join the grown-ups table."

"Ooooookay," Jake said.

Sam smacked Blake on the back.

"Now you're talking," he said. "The grown-ups

table. Hah!"

Jake was back in a flash, two bourbons in hand.

"Go slow now," he said, "there's a long day ahead."

Sam reached for his glass, clinked Blake's, and sipped.

"L'chaim," he said.

"L'chaim," Blake repeated.

"You know," Sam said, "that time Georgie and me went to Coney, my folks didn't know where the hell we were. It was a Sunday, and I was allowed to roam the neighborhood til dark. Usually with Georgie. That day, we got home late. I thought my folks would kill me. We were walking home, it was already dark, you know? And we went past the shoe store where Georgie's pop and mine worked."

Sam sipped his drink. Blake noticed his mother watching the conversation, even while her sister talked about something or other.

"Did you get in trouble?"

Sam laughed. "Eventually, sure. But when we walked past that shoe store, we looked inside and saw both our pops on the floor, tied up!"

"Tied up?"

"The store was robbed!" Sam said, now obviously feeling the alcohol, enjoying his story more by the second. His eyes, Blake noticed, were getting glassy.

Blake felt like he should be taking notes.

"First time I ever saw my father scared," Sam said. "Well, I guess he was scared on the boat coming over, but I barely remember that. Oh, yeah, there were cops, it was a real commotion, let me tell you."

"Did they catch the guys?"

"Catch the guys? Of course not. Nobody ever catches the guys."

"So what happened?" Blake felt like he was a kid now, sitting at the grown-ups table, listening as if he was ten. He couldn't believe what he was hearing.

"I guess whoever did it came for something they didn't find," Sam said. "They emptied the till, took the cash, but roughed up my pop a bit when he wouldn't give them what they came for. Poor Georgie's pop was just in the way."

Blake took a swig of his bourbon, eyed his uncle, swallowed.

"What they'd come for, Uncle Sam?"

"You know, kid, your mom over there on that box, she said you wanted to know about all our cut glass we used to have. You remember that stuff?"

Sam looked over at Blake's mother, who blew him a kiss.

"God love ya," Sam said to her, raising his glass.

"Not too much, Uncle Sam," she said.

"Don't you worry, tateleh," Sam said, "Rose will cut me off when it's time."

"I remember," Blake said. "There used to be a lot of it."

"Yeah, well, there was a whole lot more before you ever showed up. I didn't even know about it when that robbery happened. My pop had that stuff from the boat. We didn't take it over with us. I don't know where it came from. But when we got here, my brother Julie and my pop were lugging this huge thing, like a crate."

Sam caught Jake's eye again, pointed to his glass, held up a finger. Rose held Jake back, gave Sam a look, and he could tell she was saying to Jake, one more. And then she gave Sam a look, put her finger along her throat, and made a motion, like, last one! You're cut off!

"I don't understand," Blake said. "Your father somehow got the crystal on the boat?"

"Oh it was more than crystal," Sam said. "I found out much later, when I got older. I think Julie, you remember that picture you used to ask about? That was my brother, Julius. Julie."

"I remember he died in the flu epidemic."

Jake was there with a glass, which Sam reached for, but Jake pulled it back.

"Aunt Rose said next time it'll be OJ for you, Uncle Sam."

"Yeah yeah, I know," he said, taking it. "I saw her with the look. Thanks, Jakie."

"Uncle Sam, you were saying…"

"What was I saying? You remember?"

"Your brother, Julie. The crystal."

"Oh yeah," Sam said, shaking his head. "My poor brother. My folks spoke no English when they got here. My pop had a cousin in Brooklyn. We had to get to the cousin to get started here, ya see? So it was up to Julie. Getting us through all the bureaucratic rigmarole, getting us from a ship to the city to a train to his cousin. We didn't know what the hell was going on. We didn't even know where we were, really. And here were my poor folks, lugging everything they were able to take, plus us three kids. So it was all on Julie."

"And you had this huge crate of crystal?"

"Like I say, my pop didn't even know what was in it. He told me one time he knew who brought it over, he knew it was probably stolen. And there was no key. So they had to get hammers and stuff, to smash it open. I felt like I was seeing a real treasure, right in front of me."

"And then it was opened," Blake said.

"My pop couldn't touch a thing. Julie was gonna start taking something out, but my Mama held him back. She reached in, pulled out something wrapped in rags. She slowly peeled off the cloth. And then she looked at what she was holding, and held it up. I'll never forget that, all of us looking up at her hands."

"What was it? What did you see?" Blake gulped his drink.

Sam looked at Blake, winked at him.

"A Fabergé egg, how about that. Right there in this little tenement in Brooklyn. Belonging to the fucking tsar. How about that?"

"A real Fabergé?" Blake wasn't sure he heard right.

"We didn't know it then, we only saw this beautiful little thing, shaped like an egg. My Mama knew, though, it was fragile as all hell. So she re-wrapped it and put it aside. And then she got to work, with the rest."

"And there was lots of stuff?"

"A few more of those eggs, all kinds of leaded glass. Wine goblets, smaller wine glasses, shot glasses, tiny ones like thimbles on a stem, then there was jewelry, I mean, I had some kind of understanding that it was very bad that we had this, that we were sorta stuck with it. But what the hell was my pop gonna do with it all?"

Sam looked into his glass.

"And now I'm stuck with orange juice all day?" he said.

Blake waved Jake over. He made his way through the crowd of family, remembering his grandmother with noise, laughter, loud conversation. Jake took both Blake's and Sam's glasses. Blake was about to say something but Jake beat him to it.

"I'll see what I can do," Jake said. "No promises."

"Jakie," Sam said, "maybe a bagel too, with something on it."

"You got it."

And when Jake reached the kitchen, Sam leaned over and whispered to Blake, "He's good, your brother. If anyone can get me a drink out of my Rose, it's him."

"So what did your pop do?"

"Brought his cousin in, and Julie helped too. His cousin, may he rest in peace, he knew a jeweler from the neighborhood, he had this store on the same block where my pop would get a job in the shoe store. My cousin trusted this guy. He came by, looked it over, held up a necklace and said, I'll never forget, he said, this will buy you food for a year. Hah! A year!"

Sam sipped, closed his eyes, took a breath.

"Uncle Sam?"

"Blake," he said, opening his eyes, "why you want to know all this?"

Blake knew he couldn't tell Sam about the tape of his parents talking, or wanting to solve ancient family mysteries, finally getting to some truth. Not today. He just wanted to hear the stories.

"I guess, since I grew up trying so hard to never break any of that stuff, there had to be a reason why it was so special to my grandmother."

"Well Blake, that jeweler, he took a few pieces. I guess my pop figured that it was theirs, whether they wanted it or not. They certainly weren't going to the police. They'd never see that stuff again. So that friend of my pop, he sold a few, and it got my family into our first place. I guess my folks had enough for a few months rent, then my pop got the job in the shoe store. I think every now and then my pop would take a piece, have the jeweler buy it, and we'd have clothes, you know? Or some decent wine for Passover. And maybe a bottle of schnapps, you know? And I think I remember my Mama loving this new winter coat."

"Gadzooks, there must have been a lot."

Sam shrugged.

"Maybe, I don't know. Once we had our own place, Julie was in charge of it all. The trunk became like a little table, against a wall. My Mama kept a tablecloth on it, with a vase. But you know, Blake, we knew we shouldn't keep it. My pop thought the people it really belonged to, well, not really belonged to, because they probably stole it too, back in Europe, but he thought they'd somehow figure out we had it, so for a while they were always walking on eggshells."

"And then your brother died," Blake said.

Sam looked into the kitchen, searching for Rose.

When he saw her, he stared at her, without looking at Blake.

"Yeah," he said, "he died. And then I became the one in charge of all the crystal."

"Did anyone come looking for it?"

Sam faced Blake, his eyes off his Rose.

"Yeah, that's who robbed my pop's store. My pop decided we had to get it out of the apartment. By then I was pals with Georgie, and his pop was involved in some shady stuff in the neighborhood, so Georgie asked his pop, and they took it for a while. I'm pretty sure my pop gave Benny a piece from the collection, that's what we called it, the collection, for his part in hiding it. And when my sister eventually married your grandfather, he'd just bought the shirt laundry, he told my folks that they should find a better place to hide what was left, and get it out of the neighborhood, out of Georgie's house, so he made that hole in his office, and stuck what was left in there."

Blake hoped he'd remember all this. Shiva was supposed to be conversation, remembering old stories. It wasn't supposed to be full of tales that needed notes, or recordings, so he wouldn't forget. Especially when he was drinking.

"This is something," Blake said.

"I suppose," Sam said. "Some of that stuff kept us out of the Depression, y'know? My Mama always had some money for food, even when a lot of men in my neighborhood ended up in soup lines."

"Uncle Sam," Blake said, knowing he had to ask, "you said that Nana hated Aunt Rose."

"Yeah," Sam said, "like she was poison." He shook

his head.

"Why? Did it have something to do with the crystal?"

"What? Oy. No. Nothing like that. I don't think Rose knew about the crystal for a long time. I can't remember when I finally told her."

"Then why?"

Sam looked at Blake with sad eyes. His lips trembled. Blake thought, oh no, he really had too much to drink.

Sam motioned for Blake to come closer. Their heads practically touched.

"My sister, your Nana, she," Sam swallowed, "she got sick, too. You know? And Rose thinks," he wiped his eyes with the back of his hand. "Rose thinks, she said, she said..."

"What? You can tell me."

"She thinks your Nana killed my brother. And she told my sister that many times over the years. It put an ugly gulf between them, like a Grand Canyon, you know? And it never healed. Every time my Rose looked at my sister, she only saw the woman who killed my brother."

Sam looked into his empty glass.

"Shit," he said, "I need a drink. See if your brother can work me some magic, won'tcha, Blake?"

Sam handed over his glass, pulled out a handkerchief, and blew his nose.

Outburst

Sam had been holding off on bringing Rose to meet his family. He would pick her up at her house, bring her to the Levinburg dances, then walk her home. He knew, as they became more serious, that the time would come when she would have to meet his parents. He'd already not only met her parents, but had eaten at her home more than once.

A few times he surprised her by taking her to the silents, and every time they went, for Rose it was like being in a darkened theater of magic. Their first was True Heart Susie, and that's where she fell in love with Lillian Gish. She could barely blink, wanting to have every second with her eyes only on the screen, but at one point she looked over at Sam, and he wasn't watching the movie at all. He was watching her.

Her favorite was Orphans of the Storm, a story of the French Revolution, and Gish and her sister Dorothy played sisters in the film. When the lights came up Rose was surprised to find herself in an auditorium filled with people. She'd been so enraptured by the story she forgot where she was.

So when Sam picked her up, she never knew whether they were heading to a neighborhood dance, or to a theater showing some new film that would take her away as if in a dream.

One night, as he walked her home after a night of dancing, she knew she had to finally broach the subject.

"Sam," she said, squeezing his hand, "it seems we are, how would you say? A couple?"

Sam laughed.

"A couple of what?"

She slapped his shoulder.

"Stop! You know what I mean!"

He took both her hands in his, and stared deeply into her eyes.

"Rose, my Rose, yes, that is what we are. We are a couple."

They resumed their walk to her house, in the cool autumn air.

"Yes, we are, so, my dear Sam, when do I meet your family? You already know mine."

She could feel his hesitation, even in his hand that she held.

"What? What is it?"

She knew nothing of his home life, but he slowly began telling her the story of his family's coming to New York, how his brother Julius, Moshe when they left Europe, had taken charge, and gotten his family safely to Brooklyn.

He said that he and his sister were completely unable to understand the machinations of the journey, even as it finally came to an end. His father's cousin had helped them get set up, had even gotten his father a job in the neighborhood. His brother got both him and his sister into school.

So, she said, when can I meet this brother? This sister? Your parents?

Sam stopped under a streetlight. He dropped her hand. What had she said? He wouldn't look her in the eye.

"Sam, what? What is it?"

"There is only my sister. Jennie. There is no brother."

He wouldn't take her hand, and they did not resume walking. He stood and told her, in a quiet monotone, how her sister and cousin had accompanied their brother to an army base in Jersey, four years ago, where he would become a soldier, something no one in their family wanted to happen. How his sister became ill on the trip, how she had hugged and kissed their brother the day they left him alone at the training center, how Julius had spent two days there before boarding a train to Kansas, how when the train arrived at his new army base he was already sick, how he'd languished in his tent before being transferred to the hospital tent, where he lay with other young men, writhing with fever, shaking with chills, how he had died within a week of his arrival, and how he, Sam, had to go to Manhattan to meet a train that contained his brother's coffin, how he had to find a burial plot in Brooklyn, and arrange for his brother's funeral. How his family sat shiva for his brother, and the empty black hole that formed in his family by his brother's death, a hole that had never filled. And how his parents never seemed to smile again.

Rose could see his tears, glistening on his cheek by the light of the streetlamp. He wouldn't look at her, as he quietly sobbed.

"Oh my dear Sam," she said, taking him in her arms.

He stood there and cried like a child, sobbing loudly on the empty street. She held him while he moaned and let out what he'd probably been carrying with him these past years. She remembered the sickness that seemed to sweep every neighborhood, people in the streets wearing masks on their faces, neighbors and friends dying of this strange new disease. Somehow, by the grace of God, her family was spared. She had no idea why she never got sick, why her parents were still with her. And here, now, she was seeing the pain in someone she loved, who had lost a brother he worshipped, and loved deeply.

"Oh my Sam, Sam, Sam," she said, holding him while his wracked sobs shook them both.

Finally, he caught his breath, wiped his face with his sleeve, and looked away into the night's dark distance.

And then he looked at her and offered a weak smile.

"So now you know," he said. "My family is broken, my brother is gone, and I am the one in charge."

"But your sister," she said, "she got well?"

"Yes, she was in bed for a few weeks, hardly eating, it was like she was wasting away, but she slowly regained her health, found her strength, and is still with us."

He took her hand and they continued walking.

"And yes," he said, "I will bring you to meet my broken family, Rose."

They had reached her building. He faced her, leaned over and kissed her forehead.

"My Rose, my life," he said. "Next week, I'll come here and bring you to my home. You can have Shabbos dinner with my family."

"I would like that very much," she said, kissing his cheek, "I know I will not be able to fill the emptiness you say still haunts your family. But maybe when they see our happiness, maybe that will help fill it a little."

Sam was not looking forward to this meeting in the least. He knew his parents wouldn't like Rose. She had not a whit of the immigrant's aura about her. She was Brooklyn, through and through, even in the way she smoked, and held her cigarette. He thought she looked like one of the stars they saw in the moving pictures. They might just think she wore too much make-up, lipstick, mascara, rouge, things that didn't exist in his house, to cover up who she really was, whoever that might be.

His sister was the complete opposite of Rose; plain, soft-spoken, aloof. She carried with her, he knew, the anger of having brought the sickness to their brother. And she still refused to fully accept her American identity. Some days she was Jennie, but with a reluctance that was obvious. Some days she was Gdanke, especially when she spoke to her parents in Yiddish. He never knew who would greet him when he entered the house.

That Friday he picked up Rose as usual. He could tell she was trying her best to tone down her Rose-ness. She wore a plain dress, with a simple hat. Her shoes had virtually no heel. They walked slowly. He thought the slower they walked, the later they'd arrive, which meant the less time they would have to spend in his parents' bleak household.

"My mother wanted me to bring a challah," Rose said, as they approached the building. "But I said, no, Mama, Sam's mother will have a fresh challah right out of the oven that she will be proud of."

"That is true," he said. "And if it is my sister's, then all the more reason to keep your mother's at home."

They stood at the base of the stoop, holding hands, looking up at the door.

"Are you ready?" Sam said.

She didn't answer, but took the first step, and led him up the stoop. At the top she waited for him to open the door. They entered the foyer where he took her coat and hat, hung them on a peg, as well as his hat, and she followed him down a short hallway to a waiting door. They looked at each other with a quick glance, Sam's eyebrows raised a notch, and Rose nodded her head.

"Okay," he said.

The first thing Rose saw were the Shabbos candles, in the center of the table, already lit. Rose took this as an immediate affront to her being there. Sam of course told his parents he was bringing the woman he was seeing, so she assumed she would be part of the candle-lighting. But they'd started Shabbos without them.

"Hello?" Sam said. "Here we are!"

Sam took Rose's hand and brought her into the kitchen, where his mother was stirring a pot of soup. The room smelled of rich food, delicious bread, and a chicken soup that made her mouth water.

"Mama, here is Rose," Sam said.

The woman looked up, eyed Rose up and down, nodded her head.

"Sam told us all about you," she said, a spoon at her lips. She sipped.

"Your soup smells so good!" Rose said.

"Danke," Sam's mother said, "yes, thank you."

She turned to her few spices, threw in a pinch of this, a pinch of that, and stirred the pot, without looking up.

Rose looked at Sam for help. He took her hand and led her into the sitting room. His father sat in a large upholstered chair, his head in the Forward that he read with a bit too much attention.

"Papa," Sam said.

The man's eyes went not to his son, but to the woman standing next to him.

He smiled at her, and Rose felt welcome.

"This is your Rose?" he said, putting the newspaper on the floor, and standing up.

Sam stood proudly next to her, looking at her the way she loved.

"Yes, Papa, this is my Rose," he said, a sudden smile on his face opening his heart.

"Well," the old man said, "let's eat!"

And he shuffled over to the table, taking the seat at its head.

Sam thought it strange that his sister wasn't also here, ready to meet his girl. He didn't want to sit yet, so he stood with Rose as his mother came to the table, carrying the pot of soup. She gently put it down, and began filling bowls, placing them around the table. Sam's father opened a bottle of wine, and began filling glasses.

"Come, Sam, sit already!" he said.

Sam was about to ask after his sister, when she was suddenly standing beside him. He hadn't even heard her enter the room. She seemed to appear out of nowhere.

"Here she is!" Sam said, feeling completely at a loss of words in his own house. "Rose, this is my sister, Jennie. Jennie, meet my Rose."

Rose extended her hand.

"Jennie, so nice to meet you."

"Gdanke," she said, giving Rose's hand a quick shake.

"You're welcome!" Rose said, not understanding.

At that moment, what occurred in each of the two women's minds would set the tone for their decades-long relationship. Gdanke thought, this woman has nothing between her ears. Surely my brother told her my true name. And, she wears too much disgusting paste on her face and her lips. While Rose thought, this woman is like a stiff board, unfeeling, unyielding.

They all sat. Sam's father held up his wine glass, said the brief prayer, and then drank. Sam held up his glass, gave Rose a nod, and she lifted her glass as well. The whole family spent a few silent seconds sipping wine.

Rose thought, I should have had a glass or two before Sam came to pick me up.

The meal was mostly silent, the only sound that of everyone eating. Sam tried to bring up various subjects of conversation, but he would only get nods from his family, or quick one-word answers. Rose became aware, at one point, that she was sitting in the chair that used to belong to the missing son, Sam's brother. She felt like an intruder, and she saw it in Jennie's eyes.

As soon as they'd finished, Jennie stood and began stacking plates. Rose had barely taken her last bite.

"So," Sam's father said, "you go tonight to the dancing?"

"Sam, are we dancing tonight?" Rose said.

Sam beamed at her.

"Yes, I think we'll go see if there is a violin tonight," he said.

"You don't have to wait," his mother said, lifting a stack of dishes. "Go, go have your fun. Gdanke and I will clean up. Your father can go back to his Forward. Go! Enjoy."

Sam's sister was already at the sink, scrubbing a pot.

Rose looked at Sam for rescue, and he stood, got behind her chair, and gently pulled it so Rose could stand.

"Mrs. Rosen," Rose said, "thank you for allowing me to share in your beautiful Shabbos dinner. It was all so delicious."

"Danke," Sam's mother said, "good Shabbos."

Once in the hallway, Rose grabbed Sam's hand, headed to the front door, grabbed her hat and coat, and was outside before Sam had his own coat on.

They walked down the steps quickly, and at the bottom Rose buttoned up her coat, and shivered with an exhale.

"You were correct," she said, "there is a huge

sadness in your house."

"Now you know why I love being with you. You are the opposite! You are light, and gaiety, and beauty, and laughter!"

Even through her rouged cheeks, she knew she was blushing.

The Levinburg House had the usual crowd, and many were friends of Sam and Rose. That was the release they both wanted and needed. Their dancing was like a celebration, and a cementing of their courtship.

This was the routine for many Fridays. One time dinner at Rose's family, one time dinner at Sam's. A sad rigidity with little talk at Sam's. A more exuberant time at Rose's, whose parents welcomed Sam with warm open arms. And in either case, the night ending with Sam and Rose either dancing to exhaustion, or holding hands in a dark theater, caught up in the story on the silver screen.

When Sam proposed to Rose, it was not out of a movie love story. One night, walking her home after a night of dancing, he stopped under the same streetlamp where he'd told her of his brother's dying.

"Rose," he said, sweating under his nice clothes from nerves, "I think we should marry."

Rose had seen one too many Lillian Gish films. She wanted a proposal.

"Sam," she said, as her stomach fluttered, "what are you saying?"

He took her hands in his, and leaned over and kissed her red lips, holding his lips to hers for longer than he'd ever done before.

"I am saying, will you be my wife?"

He didn't kneel, there wasn't a ring, but this was close enough. She wrapped her arms around his neck and hugged him so tight he thought she'd break one of his ribs.

"Rose," he said, "I can't breathe!"

"Oh Sam," she said, "yes! Yes I will be your wife!"

They'd both wanted a Friday dinner with both their parents there, to celebrate their news, but it didn't happen. The next week was their dinner at Rose's, where she told her parents. Their good news seemed to float in the air like tiny bubbles of joy. Rose's mother cried when Rose said they were to marry. But the week after, at Sam's, Rose made the mistake of thinking, or hoping, that their news would be received with the same generous welcoming as her parents had shown.

But it was the same as before. When Sam stood at the table, and raised his glass, as if to toast, his mother looked at his father.

"What is this?" she said. "Sam, are you finished?"

"Mama, Papa, Jennie," he said, "I would like us to raise our glasses, because I have news. Rose and I will marry! Jennie, you will have a sister! Mama, Papa, you will have a new daughter-in-law!" And he drank his wine, until the glass was empty.

Rose took a sip, but no one else followed. Then Sam's father laughed, and stood as well.

"Sam," he said, "this is good news! Mazel tov!" He drank, and sat down.

"You're such a good boy," Sam's mother said. "This is what you want?"

"Mama," Jennie said. She had yet to take a sip of wine.

"Yes, Mama," Sam said, looking at Rose. "This is what we both want."

His mother gave a quick shrug.

"Okay, then, a toast," she said, and took a quick sip of her wine.

Rose would have cried, but she held in her emotions. She did not feel any more welcome at that moment than she'd ever felt at any of the other dinners at Sam's house.

Rose couldn't figure out what she had done wrong. Was it how she dressed? How she made up her face to look beautiful for Sam? Her obviously being an American from Brooklyn, and not an immigrant in a foreign land?

Sam knew something troubled Rose, and that it was his family. He tried not to let the coldness of his house affect their being together. That night, he held her closer than he ever had during one of the slow songs that played on the piano at the dance.

He saw a tear in her eye.

"My sweet Rose," he said, gliding her around the floor, "you know I care not a feather what my family thinks of you, of us. Yes?"

"Yes, I know," she said, wiping her cheek. "But I was so hoping to feel welcome, once they knew. They hate me."

"No," he said. "I think they hate life. That is not the same."

Later, bidding their friends farewell, walking back towards Rose's house, they came to a small corner store that always was open late into the night. Part candy store, part luncheonette, part news stand, the counter was usually filled at night with taxi drivers, streetcar operators just off their late shifts, and other night owls who had no reason to head home and wanted nothing more than coffee and a donut.

Passing the door to this establishment, it opened and there was Jennie, carrying a small bag that held what looked like a bottle of milk.

She and Sam both saw each other at the same moment. All three of them stopped in front of the store.

"Jennie?" Sam said.

"Mama needed milk," Jennie said, and she started in the direction of her and Sam's building. She didn't acknowledge Rose.

After maybe ten steps away from them, Rose felt, finally, like she'd had enough of this coldness.

"Why do you hate me?" she called out.

Jennie stopped, turned around, and came back to face them both.

"You think I hate you?" she said, staring daggers into Rose's eyes.

"Jennie, please," Sam said.

"No, no," Jennie said. "Answer my question, thank you."

"Are you happy that your brother has found love?" Rose said. "Are you happy that he will be married to a woman who loves him with her life?"

"I love my brother," Jennie said. "His happiness is my wish. I have no such wish for you." And as she began to walk past them, Rose grabbed hold of Jennie's coat.

Sam thought, Oy my God, what is happening here?

"Take your hand off me," Jennie said.

"I want to know what I have done to deserve your coldness," Rose said.

"You want to marry my brother? Go! Marry! I will be there to stand with my brother. Go. Take him out of our house. Leave me with my parents. I will take care of them. Me. I will be there for them. Me. I will care for them unto death."

"Like you cared for your brother?" Rose said.

Sam looked up and down the street, to make sure no one was approaching.

"What did you say?" Jennie said.

"I know what you did," Rose said. "Sam told me everything. You made your brother sick. You came home and got well. But he went alone to the middle of the country, and he took your sickness with him. And he was alone when he died. You weren't there. His parents weren't there. Sam wasn't there. But Sam had to get him when he came home – in a wooden box! Were you there with Sam? No. He had to do that alone. This was you, Jennie, Gdanke, whatever you call yourself. You did this."

Sam had no idea what to do. His eyes went from his sister to his girl. Jennie's face reddened, Sam could tell she was working her mind to find some words to counter the accusations, all true, that Rose was making. He wished now that he'd never told Rose the story of Julius's death.

"Rose, darling," he said.

"No!" Rose said, standing her ground. "I want to

hear what your sister has to say."

Sam looked to Jennie, and there were tears running down her cheeks.

"You!" she said to Rose, her voice choking on the words, "go, take my brother away. Do what you do! Go! Go! Go…." She took a breath, and raised her hand as if commanding. "Go to the Devil!" She turned, and ran down the street, dropping her bag, the bottle of milk shattering on the pavement, causing a white puddle.

Rose and Sam could hear Jennie crying, her sobs filling the street, echoing off the darkened tenements as she ran for home.

They watched her until she was indistinguishable from the shadows of the night.

Rose looked at Sam, her eyes filling with tears.

"She cursed me," Rose said, her voice rising in panic, "your sister sent me to the Devil!"

They both knew that, for an immigrant girl like Jennie, this was possibly the worst thing a person could say to another. This was not an expression. This was, indeed, a curse. The words contained a heavy weight that could never be made lighter. This curse could mean a lifetime of sickness. It could mean a horrible marriage. It could mean a dried-up womb, and no children. It could mean all of it.

"No," Sam said, holding Rose while she cried in his arms.

He knew, as well as she, that his sister's curse would follow them into the future, no matter if they lived to be one hundred, no matter if they moved as far away from this city as they could.

He held her until her sobs ebbed, until she made only small sounds of sadness. Sam lifted her face towards his, his hand gentle on her chin.

"My Rose," he said, his voice so soft she could barely hear him, "my sister's curse will fall from us to this filthy street we stand on. I will be with you always. You will always have my love."

She reached up and kissed his lips. She knew he was trying to make her – make them both – feel better.

She took his arm in hers and they continued their walk home. Neither said a word the rest of the way.

They both knew that Sam was lying. What was done could never be undone.

Georgie

So I just hafta say that I'm not sure exactly where I am.
I think I know why, but not where. It's kinda weird, see,
because this does happen now and then, and it makes me
think, how can I say it? That I'm dead? Okay then. I'm
dead. But if I'm dead, how am I here talking?

It's the candles, is what I figured out. Jews light
these candles that burn for 24 hours called yahrzeit candles,
okay? You light 'em on the date of someone's death in your
immediate family. So I grew up with my folks lighting these
candles for their folks. And then I lit 'em for my folks. And,
obviously, my kids are lighting them for me, and that's
when I sort of appear. And also lighting them for their mom,
my wife, may she rest in peace.

Listen, I never believed in no afterlife, okay? That's
a bunch of hooey. But still, when my kids, I got two kids
all grown, Jimmy and Adra, good kids, when they light
their candles, it's like, there I am, standing next to them,

or behind them. Even if Jimmy lights his in his house, and then at the same second Adra lights hers at her house, I'm in both places. How can that be? Which means, to me, that I'm no ghost. But I'm there. They can't see me. And I can't talk to them. I've tried, but no go.

So you tell me. What I think is, this is the afterlife. That's what those candles are. I'm telling you, I see them. I hear what they're saying. Jimmy has a sweet wife and they have a kid, she was my first grandkid! And I see her, too. She asked about the candles when she was small, I guess all kids do, and I heard her ask, and heard what her mom said, how it's for me. Her Grandpa. And then, when the candle burns out after the 24 hours, poof, I'm gone, I don't know where, but I'm not there where the candle is, I'm not in some new place that I can see myself in, I'm just gone. They never even know that I'm there, standing with them, watching my candle burn. But I am. And then I'm not.

I know. This doesn't make any sense to me, either.

When I was a kid, I'm talking a long time ago, in Brooklyn, I hated going to shul. My pops used to go on the High Holy Days and he'd try to drag me with him. If I was smart, I'd be out of the house early, before he even got up, so he wouldn't find me, and I'd be out somewhere, sometimes with my pal Sam, if he could escape too, but sometimes alone. And there was one time he caught me, so I had to go, and that time the Rabbi, in his High Holy Day sermon, said two things that hit me, and stuck with me, even here, in whatever this is, while my candle burns in my kids' houses. One of them I thought was dreck, you know, nonsense. The other made sense.

The first was that all us kids had to learn to say the Kaddish, which is the prayer for the dead. He said that when someone dies, like our folks, if we say the Kaddish for them, then they're written up in the Book of Life. I mean, did you ever hear something so dumb? Like, after my pops and Ma died, why would they need to be written in some book of life? How would Kaddish help them? They're dead. A lot of good it woulda done them. I don't even know if my kids ever said it for me, and here I am. At least while the candles burn.

The other thing, though, this made sense. He said that when we're dead, Jews don't believe in a heaven and hell, which sure made me breathe a sigh of relief, lemme tell you, but how we believe in the afterlife is kinda tricky. What he said, lemme see if I can remember how it went, was that, if we're remembered, presto! That's the afterlife. And if we're loved and remembered, we have a sweet afterlife. Somehow, that day so long ago in a drafty synagogue, what that guy said made sense to me. I mean, listen, I don't believe in no God, you know? Cause, y'know, if there was, don't you think I woulda seen him, considering my circumstances? But still, I show up once a year on the day I died, I see my kids lighting my candles, and poof: there I am in the afterlife.

So I don't have a lot of time right here, but I think, like I said, I know why, even though God knows (and I don't believe in God, remember?) I have no idea where the hell I am (and there's no hell either, thank God!).

It's about Sam. And Rose. And Esther, who was Rose's best friend, who I married in 1923, who was the mother of my two great kids. I wish I could see her when I appear when my candles are lit, but that hasn't happened yet, so it probably won't. But I'm sure our kids light one for her, and she was certainly loved, so at least (I hope) she's having a sweet afterlife, too.

Lemme just say that Esther was this little tiny thing, she made Rose look tall, so when we first started courting I called her Itsy Bitsy Esther, and then, I think because of Rose, who did it first, we just started calling her Bitsy, and that became her nickname.

They were some pair, those two. Rose with her red hair the color of a tomato almost, and Esther with the darkest hair I ever seen, and eyes that were so brown, almost black, both of 'em loud Brooklyn girls, smoking, laughing. The first time I looked into Bitsy's eyes, and she really looked into mine, I swear I got the shivers. But I liked those shivers. I thought, this girl I wanna know. And I guess I did, huh.

I never liked my nickname, Georgie. Probably because of that stupid kids rhyme, Georgie Porgie pudding and pie kissed the girls and made them cry? I mean, talk about a bad reputation before you say a word, right? I don't know who started it. I think maybe some aunt I had. But my Ma called me that when I was too small to argue, and it stuck. And somehow, like when I met Sam, he just started calling me that too. I kinda had my revenge in a way, once I learned to write my name in script. Script, that's what we used to call cursive, in case you didn't know. Why'd they change it to cursive, can you tell me that? So when I sign my name, I write George in script, and then, like a, what's it called, a flourish? I write a tiny 'e' in a way that looks like a backwards 3. I have to say, it's spiffy. I made it up myself. So, when I sign my name, I'm "George-e" okay? Sounds the same, but it's really my real name.

George.

So like I said, me and Sam. We were like brothers, the two of us. Well, he had a brother, who I knew for a few years, til he went west to be in the Army, got sick, and died. But after that, Sam only had his sister, Jennie. I have a sister too, may she rest in peace, and I hope she has an afterlife too, when her candle burns, but she was much older than me, and out of the house and married when I was still a kid.

So Sam and me, when we met at school, we took to each other like lox and cream cheese, or, what, peanut butter and jelly. I knew right away he was an immigrant kid. He sure looked scared. The look on his face, I knew that meant he knew probably no English at all. We used to really rag on those new kids, and sure, it probably wasn't fair, but that's how they learned to fit in. They took it, they probably hated it, they learned how to fit in, they fit in. Okay?

That first day, here's this new kid, his big brother, that was Julie, who died, brought him in. He talked to the teacher a bit, and led Sam to a seat right behind me. And then Julie was gone. I turned around, looked at this scared kid, and gave him a smile. I said, "Hey," and he said, just the way he said it I knew he had a thick Yid accent, he goes, "Hey," not even knowing what he'd just said, but I could tell he felt better.

And later, when we got out for the recess time, he stuck to me like glue. I didn't mind. I usually hung with McDougal, he was a good Mick in our class, but I sort of waved McDougal away, and he got that I was kind of taking care of the new kid, and keeping him from getting beat up on his first day.

That's how it started. I was thinking, I'll hang with the kid and he won't be so scared, and tomorrow I'll go back to hanging with McDougal. But that didn't happen. Sam was like, what, like lint on my coat. Hard to get off, always there. I didn't mind too much, except that me and McDougal used to smoke at one end of the schoolyard. Not that we were the toughs in the class, just that we were the only ones who did that. So when we went to our place and pulled out our packs, Sam was right there, the new kid.

I figured, okay kid, here's how it's gonna go. And I started telling him a few things, mostly how to try and sound like he belonged here. I didn't want to turn my smoking with McDougal into lessons about how to talk, but that's what it turned into for a while. Eventually, of course, he wanted to smoke too, so what am I gonna do, say no?

It was funny, McDougal was my only Irish friend, and I was his only Jew friend. So he got a kick out of this puppy kind of kid wanting to hang with us. A lot of days, if McDougal didn't show, it was just me and Sam. And if I didn't show, McDougal let Sam stay with him.

But eventually, it was more me and Sam, because we lived near each other, and we'd walk to school together, and then walk home together, too.

We'd get into some trouble sometimes. Like, I taught him how to steal an apple from a pushcart. Most times we didn't get caught, but sometimes we'd be chased for a block or two til the guy ran out of breath. And I showed him how

I got change for helping an old lady with her grocery bags. He almost couldn't believe that. I wanted to really make him feel like he was one of us who belonged here, and I figured the best way was to take him to Coney. And I did. And I knew that after the rides, and some Nathan's, if I took him to see the tiny babies in the incubators, he'd know, this sure ain't back home where he came from. He'd be slack-jawed, and he was.

I guess you could say that we grew up together. So when Julie died, I'd already known Sam for a few years. Julie was a great older brother. Once in a blue moon he'd take us for egg creams, and just sit there while we slobbered our mouths with white foam. I knew Sam thought the world of Julie, and when they got the news, he died of that flu that you may have read about, he and his sister Jennie couldn't deal. Their parents were wrecks, Jennie was sick too, so she was out of the picture, but Sam, I told Sam, hey, it's all on you now. You gotta pull it together, for your brother, okay?

And he did, kinda. The main thing he was so messed up about was what he called 'the collection.' He'd mentioned it a few times, but never really said what it was a collection of. He said that Julie was in charge of it, and it came with them off the boat. That night we went to Coney? We're coming back, it's already dark, we both figure we're gonna get whipped by showing up so late, and we go past our pops' shoe store, and turns out they was robbed, or at least it was an attempted robbery. My pops was pretty good with tough guys, I always thought of him as a tough guy himself, but we found both our pops tied up on the floor. First time I ever wanted to call the cops!

The next day, smoking in the schoolyard, Sam told me for the first time, really, about the collection. I thought it was just a robbery, but Sam said he heard his folks talking, and he thought that the guys who tied up our pops was looking for that collection. Sam said his folks were now scared to death to even leave the house, his Pop was sure the store would be robbed again even if it wasn't there, and now that Julie was gone, it was up to Sam to take care of it.

I almost didn't believe it, what Sam was saying. This crate they had, that was filled with all kinds of stuff, valuable stuff, they didn't bring it with them on the trip over. Sam's Pop found it on the boat. The guy who had it was someone he knew from back home who was in charge of it, and he was thrown overboard, drowned, because they wanted it, but Sam's Pop saw it and got it away to another part of the ship, and he was able to hang on to it all the way to Brooklyn. I never heard anything like this before. It sounded like a Keystone Kops comedy, except it wasn't funny. It was real.

Sam said, they knew my Pop had it. They don't know where we live, but they're gonna find out. My Mama is going nuts because it's right there, like a table. But it ain't no table, it's a crate.

So I said, Sam, you just gotta get rid of it, then.

And he said, no Georgie, it's like having money. We need it.

And I said, then we gotta get it outta there.

My pops had already heard the whole story from Max, that's Sam's Pop, and he told him that we could take it, hide it at our house. Even if they came and searched Sam's house, when they didn't find it, Max would tell them that he'd never had it, and there was the proof. They'd never figure Max was smart enough to hide it somewhere else.

And that's what happened. One night, my pops and Max and his cousin lugged that thing out of the house, into the street, and they put it on some kid's wagon they had, and wheeled it to my house, brought it upstairs, and put it in a small room that my Ma doesn't use for anything, it was just filled with junk. So this was one more piece of junk.

And for a few years we forgot about it. Those guys never came back, so I guess they figured Max never did have it.

Once we were done with school, Sam got a job in a pool hall in the neighborhood, something his folks hated. I was still working as a pin boy at a bowling alley, which was fine with me. My folks didn't care what I did, as long as I gave my Ma some of the money they paid me. I'd go play pool when Sam was working, and sometimes he'd come and bowl a game or two when I was there. So we managed to do okay for a while once school ended, we had some fun, but we wanted more fun, y'know?

We wanted to meet girls.

There was a Levinburg House near us that had these dances once a week. I figured, hey, why not? So I talked Sam into going, and there was all kinds of folks like us there, young folks, a lot we knew from the neighborhood, or the shul. The first couple of times, we just went and hung back, had a nosh, looked everyone over. But then, this one time, I saw Bitsy for the first time, and I thought, there she is. It was those eyes, like I said. I couldn't stop looking at her eyes.

She let me take her onto the dance floor, twirl her around. When she laughed, I swear, it sounded like music. And she let me walk her home. Even though she came with her friend, I didn't know at the time it was Rose, she said that she'd go home with me.

And that's how it started. Soon it was me and Bitsy, Sam and Rose. Dancing, the picture shows, whatever we did was always a great night.

Julie'd been gone for a few years, and Sam's sister Jennie never came to those dances. I knew her a little, thought she was okay, but I could tell, she still didn't really belong. Part of her stayed on that boat. This happened sometimes. Folks don't talk much English, or sometimes never learn it. They can go to stores that are all Jew owned, so they can talk Yiddish even outside the house. Sam only wanted to become like me, like even McDougal. But his sister, she wouldn't make the move. Do the work. Y'know?

And I knew she had two names. He told me her name was Jennie, but when I came over one time to get Sam for some hanging in the streets, she told me that, in her house, she wasn't Jennie. She was Gdanke. And then I understood. Okay, she's not one of the old ones that come over, the Bubbes and the Zadies, but she still wants to have one foot back home, even though this was home now. So I thought, okay, I get it. Fine with me. What did I care?

After a couple years of things sorta being the same, I got a chance to move out of the bowling alley. I knew a kid from the neighborhood, he had an uncle who was in the button business. So the kid started working there, and suddenly this kid has some real money. And he told me that there was another new business happening that he had a connection to. Zippers. Can you believe it? Now, no big deal. Zippers on pants, coats, even wallets. But back then, trust me, zippers were this new thing. He got me a job in Manhattan, and I worked my way in, and pretty soon I was moving up. Which meant more dough. My Ma was thrilled, and truth to tell, I don't think my pops ever thought I'd amount to anything. Well, I showed him.

And it got to where, being at that place a while, I started to see how things weren't done so good. I'm no genius, trust me, but I still saw where those guys were just throwing money out the window. And I told Sam. He knew I was suddenly making money. He was still stuck in the pool hall, and I knew he wanted out. So one night, I was over there, we were shooting some eightball, the place is kinda empty, and I say, out of the blue, Y'know, Sam, you don't have to keep working here. And he goes, where am I gonna go, Georgie?

And it's like I got hit with a hammer. I see it all. I say, you and me start our own zipper business. It took us a while, but that's what we did. We'd both stashed some money away, and I had an uncle who was in business upstate, and he always told me that if I needed anything, he'd come through. So we got a little loan from my unc, but we still needed a helluva lot more. It seemed like we were close, but no cigar.

One night we're sitting on the stoop, trying to figure out how to get it all done, and Sam looks at me, and he gives me a smile, like, you ready? And I go, okay Sam, what? And he says, we'll get the money. And I say, okay, how? And he says, it's in your house right now.

I think, this poor kid's been stuck in that smoky pool hall too long, and I say, Sam, you know my house. There ain't no treasure chest in there. And he starts laughing. He almost can't stop. And then I start laughing because, jeez, sure there was a treasure chest in there.

The collection.

So we go into that room, and we take all the junk off the crate, and we open it up, and I couldn't believe all the stuff in there. I'd never seen it, but Sam had, and he's rooting around, a lot of it was wrapped in rags or newspaper, but he was looking for something specific. And then he goes, here it is. And he pulls out the longest string of pearls I ever seen. I mean, it was nuts. I grabbed part of it and I thought, no way these are real. So I put them to my teeth, that's how you know. Real pearls, they feel cold. Fake feel like nothing.

Sam, I go, what the hell is it with all these pearls? And he goes, we sell the pearls, we have the money.

And to make sure we really had enough, he goes deep into the crate and pulls out a small ball of rags, and he unwraps the rag, and in the center, I swear I almost pissed myself, it was a diamond.

A fucking diamond, been there in my house the whole time.

Now I knew a few guys that Sam didn't, guys from the neighborhood who, shall we say, were getting into other kinds of business, and I say to Sam, I can sell this stuff tomorrow.

And that's how we got the rest of the money.

We actually stole some of the best guys from my company, and then stole a few accounts too. Most of the accounts at my place only knew me anyway, so when I said to them, here's how it's gonna go, you'll still deal with me, but I'll give you a better price, and then introduced Sam, it was a done deal.

Not that we were big business guys. We were both scared to death we was gonna fail. But for some reason, we didn't. I never worked so hard in my life, that first year. We had to tell the girls that for a while there would be no dancing, no movies.

Zippers. Sheesh. I mean, we were making a living.

And we told the girls, who I think saw us different. We started going up into the Bronx, to see the first talkies. When that first one with Jolson came out, I almost couldn't believe it. The guys was talking up there on the screen! And we went to some good places to eat.

Sam, I knew, really thought he'd made it. And he wanted to marry Rose.

One day, we're there in our office, I can hear the machines cranking away, we're both smoking cigars, and Sam says, Georgie, I'm gonna ask Rose to marry me. And I almost choked. I go, Sam! You devil! And he says, really Georgie, I never felt this way before. All I want is Rose. Is this love? And I put my cigar down, and I kinda stroke my chin. And I think, Sam here's getting deep on me. And I go, Sam, I think you and me both know that it's love. In fact, I think I'm in love with Bitsy.

And then he says something I never thought would happen. He says to me, Georgie, with Julie gone, I don't have my brother. But I need a best man. So would you do that for me, Georgie? Would you be my best man?

Can you believe it? I couldn't. I also couldn't believe that here he is, my best friend, telling me he's gonna marry Rose, and I'm gonna be his best man, before he even proposes to his girl! What if she says no? How nuts is this guy?

But I'm touched, like deep down, and at first I can hardly talk. But I give him a smile, and I pick up my cigar, and take a deep hit, and blow a huge smoke ring there in our office in our business that we had for forty years, and I say, Sam, you honor me and I would be happy to stand there with you on your wedding day.

That was some day. Sam started inviting everyone he knew, Rose had all her family and lots of their friends, and all our friends from the dances, and even a whole bunch that he knew just from the shul, he ended up renting the whole Levinburg dance hall, and he got all our friends who played instruments over the years to play like a real band, and there was tons of food and lots of good liquor, even though it was still Prohibition, and he paid for the whole thing by me selling another few pieces from the collection.

And the morning of the reception, in the synagogue, when he and Rose stood under the chuppah, that's the religious canopy a couple stand under, and had the actual wedding, I was there next to him, like a brother would be, a real brother, and I handed him the rings, and when he lifted the veil off Rose's face, I swear, it was like she had a light inside her that was glowing out, like something magic, and I never seen anything like it before.

And there was me and Bitsy, Bitsy standing next to Rose, me next to Sam, the four of us like our own little family, and when Sam kissed Rose, and they were married, I remember thinking, I'll never forget this, Sam catches my eye for a second, and I think, you done good, kid. You made it.

A Pat on the Head

Blake lit the candle, placed it on the stove in the kitchen, and stared at the flame. He thought he'd come to a brick wall as far as the family crystal went. Uncle Sam hadn't given him much to go on. He wasn't sure where to go next.

So he figured he'd light his father's candle, and after a few minutes start playing the tape of his parents talking to him from so long ago.

Blake got into the habit of playing the tape of his parents' voices on their yahrzeit days, while their candles burned. It made him sad, nostalgic, to hear their voices, but he still thought the same thing he'd thought for years: it no longer sounded like them. He wished he had some more recordings, to compare with what he had.

But what he heard must have been what they really sounded like, because when he hears Jake on the tape, it surely sounds like him, even though he's so much younger. Why did his memory do this to him? Or, why did the memory of their particular voices change at some point?

He's been lighting his father's candle for years now. His father died relatively young, in his mid-fifties, when Blake was still in his twenties. He hadn't married Molly yet; they were still living together, but a wedding wasn't on any kind of agenda. Usually, even before they got married, it was Molly who would tell him, "Make sure you have a candle for your father, you gotta light it on Sunday." And then Molly's parents were gone, and even though she wasn't Jewish, she liked the tradition, so she'd buy candles for her parents. Then Blake's mom died, and they always had at least four candles in the house at any one time.

Blake would light the candle, and before playing the tape, he'd stand there, in the kitchen, with the lights off, watching the flame dance in the tiny glass. He'd stare and stare, thinking about how life would have been so different had his father lived into his 80s, or 70s, or even his 60s. There were years when he'd stare at the candle and be full of anger. Other years he'd just be sad, his eyes tearing up.

If only he could tell him something to let his father know he and Jake were both okay. Hey Dad! I'm married now! So is Jake! We're doing okay! Hello? You out there, somewhere, anywhere?

But nothing. Just him in the kitchen, staring at a flame, thinking about all the years gone since he saw his parents in the flesh.

One thing that would sometimes pop into his head, whether he was feeling sad, wistful, rueful, angry, whatever, was that no matter how hard he tried, he could never evoke a memory of his father saying his name. He and his father weren't close. From the time he'd been forced into Hebrew school, forced to have a bar-mitzvah and learn all that stuff, even at his father's funeral, he felt like there was something that always kept them apart.

He knew Jake didn't feel this way. Jake was so much like their father, from their love of sports, to their senses of humor, which could be crass at times, to even how they ate a sandwich. Blake had plenty of memories of Jake and their dad having a catch, arguing about a Super Bowl, watching a World Series together. If there was a memory that included Blake, it was always him joining them after something had started. He'd get his glove to make it a three-way catch. He'd fetch beers while a game played on TV. But he always felt like an outsider, in his own family.

He's positive: his father never called him by his name.

Even on that tape, he says, "Hiya, fella," and during his childhood, the main name he'd be called by his father was Boy.

Hey Boy, could you open a beer for the Old Man?

Hey Boy, take the dog out.

Boy, go help your Mom in the kitchen.

Hey Boy, can you get me a little ice cream?

When he was a small kid, it never occurred to him that his father should be calling him Blake. Or even Son. As he got older, especially into his rebellious hippie years, it made him more and more upset, this feeling of remoteness when it came to his father.

He did understand, though, that part of this was the generation of men his father was part of. During the

'50s and '60s, he knew, from talking of this with other men friends, the role of a successful father was to provide for his family. Food on the table, clothes, shoes, a warm house in winter. A place to lay one's head.

A few years after Blake moved to Colorado, he joined a 'men's group,' as they called it, and met five other men his age, from different economic backgrounds, different parts of the country, but over the years of meeting with these men, they all eventually came to similar beliefs about their fathers: emotional closeness had very little to do with any of their families of origin, at least as far as their fathers were concerned.

He also knew that his father's role in World War II contributed to his aloofness. His father, he later learned from his mother, had seen a lot of death in the war, perhaps too much for anyone to handle. When his father died, and Blake had to provide his father's Army discharge papers in order to get the veteran's flag he was entitled to, it said, under his father's "occupation" during the war: machine gunner. His father had apparently killed many enemies: Germans or Italians. His mother once said something about his father that he'd so wanted to ask him about, but he'd never gotten the nerve. His mother said that after a few months, once some of the men in his battalion had been killed, when replacements came in, his father could look into the eyes of the new recruits, and he knew immediately which men would survive, and which would die. "If he saw death in their eyes," his mother had said, "he'd stay away from them. And he was always right."

Somehow his father had been able to tell his mother

that. He wished he could've been a fly on the wall for that conversation.

What kind of talent was that? How did his father know this? As a young man, he'd so wanted to know the answers to these and other questions. But he could never bring himself to broach such subjects that were obviously filled with dread, fear, horror. Had his father lived into a ripe old age, he believed, there might have come a time, when Blake was middle-aged, maybe over a drink or a few drinks, he could have tried to understand how war breaks young men in such a way that they never truly come back to themselves, but are always an arm's length from being comfortable in their own skins.

Blake knew from his mother, who told him many things about his father when he was a teenager and first expressing his feeling of not even being his father's son, even though it was undeniable, they looked so much alike, that, yes Sunshine (her nickname for him, which, though not his name, seemed sweet and a good substitute for Blake), your father loves you very much. He loves both his sons. Don't let it get to you that he may not demonstrate it the way you want. He just may not be able to.

There were two ways, though, that he felt his father's caring, his father's faltered skimpy attempts at demonstrating to his young sons his love. And his memories of being a young boy and receiving such attempts were warm. It was only as he got a bit older that he saw these efforts as cold, distant, unloving.

The first was when he'd cry as a kid. Whether a skinned knee, a bee sting (he'd been stung a couple of times), or some other injury or even indignity that caused tears, his father always had the same quick reaction. He'd reach into his rear pants pocket, pull out his handkerchief, and delicately wipe Blake's face, absorbing his tears. He'd gently run the cloth over Blake's eyes, dabbing his eyelids, and, if there was an intense emotional upset that needed to be assuaged, he'd hold the handkerchief to the small boy's nose, and say, "Blow." Blake would blow his nose into the waiting whiteness of the handkerchief, and as his father put it back into his pocket, he always felt better.

Always.

He felt taken care of, safe, protected.

Was that a good father, in the 1950s? One night, at his men's group, as they went around the circle sharing the stiffness of their father's emotional lives, one of his "brothers," as they referred to each other, said, "Y'know, those guys, they had no clue, but they tried their best, don't you think? And so it's up to us to do better, and do our best."

Okay, he thought, I can give him that, I guess.

The second way his father showed affection was far less of a demonstration of any kind of caring, protection, or love. But it had been the only thing in Blake's (and Jake's) boyhood that showed in any way that, sure, maybe this damaged WWII vet who saw too much death, yes, loved his sons.

His father would occasionally give him a pat on the head. Sometimes, rarely, also a soft stroke of his hair.

On more severe occasions, a combination one-two: the handkerchief drying tears, a pat on the head, to close the deal.

You're okay, I'm here, I love you, my sweet son, Blake.

One night at the men's group, one of the guys said, when they'd been talking about their families of origin, if you think of how deficient our dads were, men of that generation, imagine what it must have been like to be of the generation before: the fathers of OUR fathers.

Blake got it right away. His memories of his paternal grandfather were few, but he knows he never saw his grandfather smile, or laugh. He was a stoic man of few words. He would sit his grandsons on his lap, let them pull his earlobes, but he'd give very little back. What would it have been like to have such a father in the 1930s, 1940s? He had no idea.

And he sensed that, like his father, his grandfather never told his father that he loved him. Because although he could somehow think that being called Boy instead of his name showed some emotional connection, and a handkerchief to dry his tears was comfort, and a pat on the head was affection, the absence of the three words that, to Blake, showed a true and deep connection, heart to heart, life to life, loomed huge as he grew from a boy to a teen to a man.

I love you.

He never heard these words said by the man who'd given him life, who'd provided for him his whole childhood, who, though damaged by being a machine-gunner killing other men in hellish battles, had tried in various ways to still show a bit of his humanity to his sensitive and inquiring young son. Those efforts might have been received as offered when young, but became (assumed) proof of no love at all as he got older, got rebellious, and finally left the city he'd grown up in to move half a country away, to where he'd find his own love, and eventually, hopefully, have his own family and be able to show his kids what a truly loving father should be capable of.

He'd decided, early on, long before he could actually take off and create his own life, that he would be better. He promised himself, and some unborn human that he might one day beget, to demonstrate with words, actions, hugs, kisses, laughter, his deepest feelings, the contents of his heart, his hopes, dreams, and pride in and for, whoever would one day spring from his loins (and from Molly's womb!).

And he wondered, now, staring at his father's candle, in his darkened kitchen, if his father had made some kind of promise to himself, before Blake was born. Or even after, when a new tiny human with so many needs was first brought home from the hospital.

Maybe his father had kept his promise after all.

Blake looked around the kitchen, as shadows danced on the walls from the yahrzeit candle.

Did you, Dad? he thought. Did you keep that promise to yourself?

Molly came into the kitchen and stood beside him, both of them staring at the candle's flickering flame.

"You miss him," she said.

"Yeah," he said. "There's so much I never got to tell him, you know?"

"I do," she said. "But you can still tell him."

"I can?" he said, laughing

"Yes," she said. "I believe he'd hear you."

"I don't know," he said.

"It doesn't matter," she said, "whether you believe it or not. What matters is that you tell him."

She kissed his cheek and left him to his musings, his staring.

Becoming Jennie

Jennie didn't recall her conversation with her mother, when she was a young girl, about whether she would ever marry, but over the years, especially once she saw her brother Sam so happy with Rose, who she cared for not a whit, she had her doubts that she would ever find someone.

She had little interest in the kind of social life Sam had, going to the movies and spending nights at the Levinburg dances. She liked her home; well, her parents' home. If she gave herself an opportunity to think about whether she'd ever have her own home, her thoughts only brought sadness.

Seeing Sam and Rose in the synagogue, under the wedding canopy, made her feel even more protective of her older brother than she usually felt. As Rose placed the ring on Sam's finger, Jennie thought, if you don't treat him well, you will have to deal with me.

And once Sam and Rose moved into their own

apartment, she felt more alone than ever. Her parents tried to make her happy with special events. They took her to the Folksbiene Yiddish Theater a few times, where they would see musicals, drama, even lectures, in Yiddish. In the spring they'd go to the Brooklyn Botanic Garden to enjoy the warmth and beauty of the scenery. But Jennie knew these outings were attempts to allay her loneliness. She appreciated these loving gestures, but they ultimately left her feeling even more wanting of what she didn't have.

She did take one class at the Levinburg House, where she learned to knit, and she would spend many afternoons sitting at the window, her knitting needles clicking away as she made scarves and sweaters for her and her parents. She would make such things for Sam and Rose for Chanukah. She enjoyed the repetitiveness of the craft, and it relaxed her. Her father never questioned any expense associated with her new interest. He would buy her patterns, skeins of wool, whatever she wanted, because he only wanted her to have a life as full and joyous as his son's.

One day she was sitting in her knitting chair, as she thought of it, when the door burst open and Sam and Georgie came into the house, seemingly unaware of Jennie's presence, as they were obviously in the middle of an emotional conversation.

"I don't care, Georgie," Sam said, "there has to be another way!"

"Listen, Sam," Georgie said, "my father put his foot down. Someone came into the store yesterday asking about the collection."

"You don't know that's what the guy was talking

about!"

"Then what do you think he meant? He came right out and said it. 'Enough is enough.' That's what he said. 'It's somewhere. We want what's left.' What else could he mean?"

Jennie hadn't heard a word spoken of the collection in a few years. She continued her knitting, but tried to absorb every word.

"If we bring it back here, I think my mama would faint at the thought."

"Sam, this man scared my father. I'm glad your father was at Barney's having lunch. He would have told that guy everything, and they'd be at my house in a flash. We have to move it."

"Why not at my house? Or yours?"

"I don't want Bitsy involved in any of this."

"I understand. I feel the same way about Rose."

They both looked at Jennie, seeming to notice her at the same time.

"Are you going to bring it back here?" Jennie said, putting her needles in her lap.

"Jennie, Gdanke," Sam said, going to her, kneeling before her, taking her hands in his. "I don't know what to do. But we have to do something."

She kissed his hands, stood, and went into the kitchen. Sam and Georgie followed her, as she filled the tea kettle and put it on to boil. She brought three cups to the table. Then she returned to the kitchen and emerged with a few rugelach on a plate. They watched her as no one said a word. Sam looked at Georgie, who shrugged. The two men sat. Jennie made the tea, brought it to the table, filled the cups, and sat with them.

"We know the value of what's still in the collection," she said, taking a tentative sip of her cup. "It must stay in the family."

Sam hadn't expected this. He lifted his cup and blew on his tea. George took a rugelach, shoving the whole pastry into his mouth.

"Do you think," he said, chewing loudly, crumbs falling onto his chin, "we could bring it here, just for a while?"

"Georgie, please, not with your mouth full," Jennie said, sipping her tea.

Sam laughed. Did he eat like this when he was home with his new wife?

"We used to keep it in the small room in back," Sam said. "Would we even have to tell Mama and Papa?"

Jennie thought for a second.

"Papa must know," she said. "It's here because of his foolishness, on the boat. He stole something that did not belong to him, or even to those who had it. Everything having to do with that collection is a dishonesty."

"But it helped us get established," Sam said.

"Yes," she said, "it did. So Papa must be told. Mama, I think we can bring back the crate and tell her it's now empty. She'll know we're lying as soon as we say the words. More dishonesty. But she will accept it."

"Yes, you're right," Sam said.

"My father wants it gone, today. If he comes home from the store and it's in his house, I think he'll put it out on the street for anyone to take."

Sam chewed his rugelach, took a sip of tea. He looked at Jennie, but he spoke to Georgie.

"I think, maybe, we can give your father something as a thank you for letting us hide it in his house. I know he likes the crystal."

Jennie nodded to Sam.

Sam looked at Georgie.

"He can pick whatever he likes."

Georgie nodded, his eyes going from Jennie to Sam.

"I have a friend who can help me bring it here. But it won't be today. He owes me a favor, he won't ask any questions. But today is out."

"Tomorrow, then," Jennie said. "Mama spends the morning at her shopping. Papa is at the store with Benny. Only I will be here."

Georgie reached over and put his hand on Jennie's. She blushed, looking at their two hands.

"Thank you, Gdanke," he said. "I promise it won't be here for long."

Jennie smiled.

"How do you know such a thing, Georgie?"

He laughed.

"I don't," he said. "But how do we know anything? Maybe I hope, maybe I pray, maybe it's luck. Maybe, who knows, it's God."

They sipped their tea and ate their rugelach in silence, all avoiding each others' eyes.

Jennie cleared the table and went back to her knitting, her way of saying the conversation was over. Sam and Georgie didn't say goodbye. They left, as suddenly as they'd arrived. Jennie watched them out the window as they walked down the street.

The next day Jennie was nervous. She vaguely remembered the day her Papa and Georgie's father took the crate away. She'd had nothing to do with it then. Now she was intimately involved in something she really wanted nothing to do with.

She was up with her parents, had breakfast with them, watched her father head out to the shoe store, and helped her mother clean up the table. She thought if she busied herself she wouldn't think of Georgie showing up with his friend, lugging the huge crate into the house. But it wasn't working.

She decided to escape her thoughts the way she usually escaped her life, by knitting. Once she sat in her chair and picked up the needles, she felt calmer.

Completely lost in her stitching, she lost track of time. She realized her mother was standing before her, waiting to be acknowledged. She looked up.

"I'm doing my shopping, tatelah," her mother said, using the endearment Jennie loved. "Would you like to come with me today?"

Jennie thought that her mother must know something was up.

"Not today, Mama," she said, holding up her wool. "See? I am nearing the end of this sleeve. I'd like to finish it today. Do you think Papa will like it?"

Her mother smiled at her daughter, wanting so much more than for her to be knitting sweaters.

"Yes, I think he will love this one," she said, wrapping a scarf around her head.

With her mother gone, Jennie's knitting was no longer a distraction. She couldn't go on. So she sat, staring out into the street, her mind blank, waiting for Georgie.

Before long she saw him down the street, walking with a stranger. She had no idea how long she'd been staring out the window. Georgie and his friend were carrying the crate. She could tell its weight was a strain for both of them.

She heard them enter, heard them walking down the hall. There was a knock on the door. She was up in a blink, and opened the door to the two men, each breathing heavily, the crate between them.

They didn't speak, but hefted the crate and carried it into the house. Jennie led them to the back room, where she'd cleared the space where the crate had originally lived. They placed it on the floor, Jennie had an old tablecloth handy, draping it over the ancient wood. She placed an ashtray on top along with an old copy of one of her magazines. Georgie nodded.

They came back into the living room. Jennie waited for what would come next.

"Jennie, thank you again. This is my friend I was telling you about. Irvin, here is Jennie."

The man extended his hand. At first Jennie didn't know what to do. Did he want her to take his hand? She did.

"Gdanke," she said, shaking his warm hand.

He smiled at her, but wouldn't let her hand go, though she tried to pull away.

"Which is it, then?" he said, his eyes sparkling. "Are

you Jennie? Or Gdanke?"

This made her blush. She looked at the floor for help. The floor had nothing to say.

"Whichever," she said. "I mean, whichever you like."

"Were you Gdanke before you came to America?" Irvin said.

"Yes," she said, unsure of what this man was getting at.

"Well then," he said, "since we are in America, I will be happy to make your acquaintance, Jennie."

"Okay then!" Georgie said. "Now that we all know each other, Jennie, I was telling Irv here that you made some delicious rugelach that maybe you could bring out while we discuss what we need to discuss."

Jennie wasn't prepared for this.

"Please, only if it's no trouble," Irvin said. "But after our long trek with that perilous weight, I think I would need a minute or two to rest before Georgie and I continue on our way."

"Well," she said, "I do have a few pieces left."

"Okay then!" Georgie said. "Have a seat, Irv. I'll help Jennie in the kitchen."

The two of them left Irvin sitting alone while Jennie went about filling the tea kettle, putting a few pastries on a plate, getting out cups. She thought once the crate was put away and out of sight, her nervousness would abate, but she still had flutters in her stomach.

"I'm sorry," Georgie said, "I thought we'd just leave, but I needed a moment to sit."

"How do you know this Irvin?" she said.

"He's a distant cousin of my mother," Georgie said. "I've known him my whole life. And now he's successful in business, and has a heart of gold."

"What business?" she said.

"A shirt laundry," Georgie said, "in Bay Ridge."

"A shirt laundry?" Jennie said, intrigued.

"Yeah, he's doing very well. Come, you can ask him yourself."

One thing Jennie had never learned in her years in Brooklyn was how to 'make conversation,' especially with a stranger, and especially a stranger who made her blush. But she followed Georgie back into the small dining room, where Irvin waited patiently, his hands flat on the table.

He stood as soon as he saw Jennie, and waited while she poured tea. George grabbed a rugelach as soon as he sat, and put it in his mouth, watching his friend as he tried to make Jennie feel comfortable in her own house.

"Thank you for letting us have a few minutes to rest," Irvin said, sipping his tea.

"Please, it is nothing," she said.

"Oh, it is actually something," Irvin said. "Georgie has told me a little about the journey of that huge thing we just lugged through the street. Maybe it can rest here until its final destination is decided."

"Let us hope it is soon, that final destination," she said.

They sat, they sipped, they ate Jennie's rugelach. She had no idea what to say, but she liked this Irvin and hoped he and Georgie would somehow stay for a second cup of tea. The silence was becoming oppressive, but Georgie put his cup down, as if he was reading Jennie's mind.

"You know, Jennie, Irvin is one of our friends we see at the Levinburg dances," he said.

"Yes," Irvin said, as if he'd been given permission to speak. "I don't go all the time, but it's great fun."

"That's very nice," Jennie said, "Sam met Rose there."

"Perhaps you'd like to join our little group sometime," Irvin said, "see the fun for yourself."

Jennie put her hand to her mouth, covering a smile.

"Oh no," she said, "I don't ever dance."

She pronounced it, 'dence,' rhyming with 'fence.' Irvin seemed amused by her accent.

"Well," he said, giving her a wink, which made her flutters flutter even stronger, "we don't have to dance. We can have a nosh, watch the others do the dancing."

"Oh, I don't know," she said, unable to say another word. Georgie saved her again.

"But I do know!" he said. "It's settled then. Irv will come here after your Shabbos dinner with your parents, escort you to Levinburg, and Sam and Rose and Bitsy and me will be there, waiting for you!"

"I will?" Irv said. He looked at Jennie, and they both smiled at the same time.

"Sure! It'll be fun, or, maybe, more fun than usual," Georgie said. "Will you join us, Gdanke?"

She picked up her teacup and put it to her lips, taking a quick sip, and looked at Irvin.

"I don't think Gdanke will be going," she said, "but

I think Jennie would be happy to join you."

Jennie had never experienced the kind of excitement that filled her, waiting for Irv to come and take her to the dance. She only wanted the dinner to end, so she could leave her parents alone with the Shabbos candles burning. She told her mother that a friend of Sam's was coming to bring her to the dances that Sam had been going to.

"A man?" her mother said. "Coming to take you?"

"Who is this man?" her father said, a hint of protection in his voice.

"His name is Irvin," Jennie said, "I met him the other day."

"What other day?" her mother said.

"Mama, when you went to the market."

"A man came here to meet you when I went out?"

Jennie didn't want to tell her mother about the crate now hidden again in the back room. Although she had a feeling her mother already knew this.

Struggling to find the words that would calm her mother, she was saved by a loud knock on the door. She ran to answer it.

Opening it, there was Irv, looking, to Jennie, as dashing as any man she had ever seen. He carried a small bouquet of flowers. He doffed his hat and made a small bow.

"Good Shabbos, Jennie. Are you ready to see the fun that your brother has been having all this time without you?"

Jennie nodded, because words failed her, but she managed to reach out for the flowers.

"Oh no," Irv said, "I'm afraid these are not for you."

He stepped into the apartment, and stood before both her parents, side by side with faces of stone. He held out the small bouquet.

"Mrs. Rosen," he said, handing her the flowers, "I hope you will allow Jennie to accompany me tonight to the Levinburg dance. I promise she will not be home late."

Her father raised his eyebrows, as his wife took the flowers. She instinctively brought them to her face, inhaling the sweet fragrance. She turned to her husband.

"He brought flowers. For me!" she said.

Jennie had her coat on and was waiting by the door. She couldn't get out fast enough.

"And Mr. Rosen," Irv said, extending his hand, "I wish you and your wife a very good Shabbos."

The two men shook hands.

"We will be off then," Irv said, leaving Jennie's parents standing, mute, completely intoxicated by this handsome, polite, man.

Jennie had heard of the dances since Sam first started going, but actually being there was completely different. That night there was a banjo and violin in addition to the player piano, and there were many faces she recognized from the neighborhood. She had never seen anyone dance these new American steps, and it was a kind of joyous gathering she never imagined.

Irv led her to the table that was filled with all kind of food: sliced challah, various pastries, the new snack called Wise Potato Chips, which she had only heard about, bagels, sliced lox, plates of herring, olives, sliced tomatoes, cookies, rugelach, sliced chocolate babka.

"All this food," Jennie said.

"Can I make you a small plate?" Irv said.

"But I just had dinner," she said.

"Then I will make you a dessert," he said, filling a plate with sweets.

He led her to the empty chairs that lined one wall, and they sat. Sam and Rose saw them right away, and came over.

"Can I believe what I'm seeing?" Sam said. "My sister, here in Levinburg?"

"Sam, please," she said.

"Let her be," Rose said. "Come Sam, dance with me."

And they were off to the floor, moving in ways Jennie didn't think her brother could move. She never thought she'd think it, but she appreciated her sister-in-law taking her brother away, so she wouldn't have to talk to him about being here with Irv.

"I'm afraid I don't dance," she said, nibbling a cookie.

"Tonight I don't care," Irv said, reaching for a rugelach from her plate, "I only wanted your company. We can sit and watch the others. But there may come a time when I will teach you."

"And there may come a time when I will want to learn," she said, her eyes going back to the dance floor.

She could feel his eyes on her as she watched the dancers.

Is this how it happens? she thought, as music swelled and filled the room.

And indeed, that is how it happened for Jennie. She looked forward to the next Friday with more excitement than the first time, now that she knew what to expect. Like the first time, they sat together while most of the others danced to the music. And like the first time, he walked her home before it ended, to be sure she got in before her parents became worried. And like the first time, he walked her to her door, took her hands in his, and thanked her.

But the third time, he drew her close at her door, and planted a kiss on her cheek. She thought she would faint.

The fourth time, he kissed her at the bottom of the stoop, and they both knew her parents were watching from behind a curtain. And then there was the second kiss at her door.

The fifth time, they didn't go directly to her house. They walked the neighborhood, holding hands the whole time, as they talked about their lives, Jennie explaining how she never felt like she belonged in Brooklyn, still missing her home in Europe, Irv talking about the risks he'd taken buying a laundry, procuring loans, full of trepidation in his first years until he'd achieved success.

The sixth time, Irv did not simply arrive to take Jennie to the dance. This time, he was invited to join her family for the Shabbos meal. And, like every other time, Irv had a small bouquet for her mother, to adorn the dinner table.

Then there were the High Holy Days, requiring days spent in the synagogue, and the Levinburg dances didn't happen for a few weeks. Jennie saw Irv at the religious services. They stood together in the lobby of the synagogue during one of the breaks, and she felt like she belonged somewhere, finally, for the first time, standing by his side.

The next Friday he came to take her to the dance, and she thought, tonight, tonight she would finally tell him her one secret, about the crate he'd helped Georgie bring to her home, the collection, and the burden it placed on her, and the anxiety both her parents had about owning such a thing.

For the first time, Irv didn't simply walk her home, or through the neighborhood, to share more talk, and learn more about each other. This time, Sam insisted that they all go to Barney's candy store for a cup of coffee, to extend their evening together beyond the dance. Jennie was nervous to be with the others in the company of Irv even though, by now, it was so obvious that they had become a couple.

But she said yes.

Barney always stayed open late on the weekends, and many couples ended up there, either at the counter or at one of the small tables in the back. Tonight it was unusually empty, and when they sat at the table, theirs was the only one occupied.

Sam brought back a tray of cups and a coffee pot. He filled the cups and took great joy in seeing his sister so clearly happy in the company of Irv.

As the others commenced to do their small talk, Jennie thought, this is how it is done. We are three couples, those four are married, we had a night out having fun, and now we are here, having coffee, talking about nothing at all.

But the subject soon changed to something, not nothing.

"Sam," Georgie said, as Bitsy watched him, knowing already what he was going to say, "I think it's time we said what we were going to do at some time, but some time, I think, is now."

Bitsy nodded her head, thinking, thank God. Finally.

"You mean that crate," Irv said.

"Yes," Sam said. "We have to move it. Somewhere safe. Somewhere no one would ever think to look. And then my Mama will have a good night's sleep."

Jennie thought she would be telling Irv about the crate and its dark history tonight, on the walk home. But he seemed to know about it already. Did he know all about it the day he and Georgie brought it back to her house, the day they met?

"We can't bury it," Georgie said, "because we're not pirates."

"But it is treasure," Sam said.

"I may have a solution," Irv said.

"What? Irv? You?" Jennie said, hoping he wouldn't be part of any solution.

"Tell me," Georgie said.

"My laundry," Irv said. "It's huge. I'm sure we could find a place there."

"But you have a large number of workers," Sam said. "Won't one of them find it?"

"I have an office, it's on a different floor than the laundry itself. It's small. Only I go up there. No one else is allowed. And no one else has the key."

"Do you have a safe up there?" Georgie said.

Jennie couldn't believe she was hearing this

conversation. She looked at Bitsy and Rose. Rose caught her stare and shrugged, as if to say, this is men stuff. We just listen and drink our coffee.

"No," Irv said.

"Then how can we hide it in your office?" Sam said.

"I've been up there," Georgie said. "Those walls are made of large bricks. That building is very old."

"Okay," Irv said, "I know how old my laundry is. I know the bricks."

"So we hide it in the wall, behind the bricks," Georgie said.

"That's good," Sam said.

"But there's no hole, behind any bricks," Irv said.

Georgie took a long drink of his coffee. The others watched him, as he carefully lowered his cup, wiped his mouth with a napkin, and looked from one of them to the next.

"Then we make one," he said.

Molly

When Molly met Blake, the last thing she wanted was a boyfriend. At that particular point in her life she needed alone time. She'd had a bad break-up with a guy she was seeing for about a year, they'd even lived together for a few months, but she was more and more unhappy and it felt good to let that relationship die. She liked being by herself. She had her friends, and her job at the restaurant where she'd met that boyfriend, but she got to where she thought maybe she was done with any kind of hook-up. The last thing she needed, right then, was men, even though her best friend Marcie had tried to set her up with a couple of guys. Men. Phooey.

That's where she was before Blake showed up.

It wasn't technically a blind date. There was a party, lots of people she knew, and apparently many of Blake's friends, too. This was in their college town back east. They talked a bit, but he'd made no real impression. So she was surprised when her new roommate (she kept the apartment while her ex found new digs) asked her if she'd be into having a drink with that guy from the party, she was his friend and knew he was kind of lonely. She thought, that is so teenage wasteland! That is so middle school! Using her roomie as a go-between. What the fuck?

She said fine, he could call her. But he didn't. He texted. They made a vague plan to meet at a bar they both knew.

So there they were, strangers with mutual friends, sitting in a bar, both obviously uncomfortable. She was already on her second margarita. Blake made a comment about how food was important if they were going to drink. She rolled her eyes, but didn't want to seem like she was judging him. He was just being a nice guy. Sure, let's have some nachos.

He drank bourbon and she thought for a second, hmm, wonder if tequila and bourbon will mix? He did more talking than she thought he'd do. So many guys she went out with over the years, including the ex, didn't know their way around a conversation. This guy here was an assistant professor, which in her mind meant not a real professor but a pawn in the system, underpaid and overworked. Still, that meant he had a brain and probably knew how to use it.

They did the usual dance, throwing out bits of their lives. He said he had a younger brother whose named rhymed with his. Jake. Then he rolled his eyes. Like a vaudeville act, you know?

She had one older brother, so just the two of them, like him.

They ate their nachos, sipped their drinks. She looked around the bar for anyone she might know, thinking, I might need an escape hatch from this guy. Whenever her eyes came back to him, he was just looking at her.

At one point she said, you look like you never saw a woman before.

And he said, well, I never saw a woman like you.

She could see he was fooling with her. Or else this, to him, was flirting. She downed her drink, ate the last of the chips, gave him a hard stare.

He threw back the last of his bourbon, put a twenty on the bar and said, let's take a walk.

He helped her on with her coat. So he has some manners too, she thought. Or, help her on with a coat and it'll be easy to help her out of it later.

She still didn't really trust him, but only because she didn't really know him. He was obviously treating her with true respect, and she could tell he was acting like this was a very delicate encounter, one he didn't want to end.

They walked the neighborhood. He talked, she listened, she talked, he asked questions, so he was listening as well. At one point he took her hand and she thought, that's nice. They strolled, hand in hand, the conversation drifting. Whenever she thought they had a nice thread going, he'd change the subject and they'd be off on something else.

Maybe he has some kind of cognitive problem, or he's on the spectrum, his mind doesn't work linearly, she thought. When she changed the subject, he seemed confused, which confirmed for her that he was off in some way. Or maybe he wasn't a good listener after all.

Then he stopped talking. He'd made no move on her, just held her hand. They walked a couple of blocks in silence. Was he thinking how to get her back to his place? Or her place? She had her diaphragm in her purse, so if something happened she'd be ready, but she thought nothing would happen. He seemed like a nice guy, if a bit shy, a bit too much in his head.

When he started talking again, it was almost a whisper. She had to lean in to hear him. He started telling her about his most recent relationship, how it ended badly, how he thought he'd never be with anyone again. The last thing he needed was a girlfriend.

He gave her a glance, and smiled.

So why'd you ask me out? she said. Oh, he said, I heard good things about you. Like what, she said. Basically, he said, you're not psychotic.

That's good, she thought. But what does he know? This made her laugh. She stopped walking, and laughed some more. He looked at her in a way that made her think of a confused puppy, his head to one side.

Sorry, she said.

No, he said, it's okay.

They stood there, facing each other. She thought he was going to kiss her, right under the streetlight. She thought to close her eyes, but didn't.

Can I ask you something, he said.

Sure, she said.

Can I kiss you?

She'd never been asked permission before. Why would he ask permission? Who asked permission for a kiss?

Apparently this guy. Was this respect? Fear of rejection? She gave it a second's thought. What if she said no? Would he just walk away? She didn't want that, at least not yet.

Sure, she said. Sure you can.

The cliché is 'the rest is history,' but it didn't seem that way at the time. He walked her to her place, kissed her one more time, a bit less timidly, and then turned to head home. She walked maybe three steps to her door, was fumbling for her keys, when she heard him and turned around. He'd run back to where she was standing, out of breath.

Are you okay, she said.

He held up a hand, took a breath, and said, I don't know if you'll want to see me a second time, but I wanted to say that, no matter what this is, I just hope to see you again, even if we're just friends.

Who is this guy, she thought. But she said, come on in, I'll make us some tea.

They weren't apart for the next ten days. They slept together that night, but didn't have sex. They just held each other, falling asleep in each other's arms. When she opened her eyes in the morning, they'd drifted on the bed and were separated. She looked at him sleeping and thought, this could be the best date ever.

What stirred him awake was the smell of coffee. He looked around and thought, oops, why am I alone? But she was there in a sec, standing in the doorway, with two cups.

"I went and got bagels," she said. "You were sleeping so deeply I didn't want to disturb you."

And he thought, this could be the best date ever.

They moved into a new place in a few weeks, with Marcie taking the second bedroom.

They lived together in that apartment for a year.

And when he suggested they might be ready to leave this city, and said he had an old friend who was moving to Colorado, she said, I have an old friend there too. I bet we could crash with her until we get set up.

They'd had one Christmas together, and one Chanukah. She'd never had a Jewish boyfriend, nor a guy from New York, and it took her a while to get used to his loud expressive ways. The first time she met most of his family was at a birthday party for his father. They'd taken their first trip back to New York since landing in Colorado. She didn't realize how much she was craving acceptance from his family until her second drink. She believed she was being judged. No one really talked to her. But everyone talked, at once, and loud. She'd been to parties with her extended family in Albany with twice as many people, and it was three times as quiet as this mob.

He came over to where she was to ask her if she was okay, and she pulled him into a small den and shut the door.

"Are you okay?" he asked, concerned.

"They're all screaming at each other!" she said, choking on tears.

Instead of explaining the obvious mass anger of all those people she didn't know, he laughed.

"No," he said, "they're not screaming. They're talking. This is my family. This is them having a great time. Come on, I'll teach you."

And he brought her back in and made sure she got

a few words in.

She got better at that over the years.

It also took her a while to understand that he had another relationship as important as the one he had with her: his writing. He'd been struggling with a novel, had had a few poems published, and was working one day at his desk, pounding away on his 1890 Underwood typewriter, when she snuck up on him and wrapped her arms around him in a bear hug.

"What are you doing?" he said.

She didn't answer, but left the room, slamming the door, upset, insulted, demeaned.

He slapped himself and snapped out of his reaction, and went to her, and tried to explain, hoped it made sense. He said that his writing was like channeling, or like being on a frozen lake where the ice was too thin to stand. One false step and he'd fall in and drown. But he always had to find his way back to the shore.

She didn't quite understand, but after that she always left him alone when he was pounding those keys.

She knew about his fascination with the family crystal. It was so clear that this was one part of his family that was buried in evasion, if not outright lies. When he told her, after years of being together, that he intended to find the truth, with the last relatives still alive from that generation, she knew he would, and that it would somehow become his next book.

She also knew about the recording of his parents, because they were together when that tape arrived. She loved hearing his parents' voices. What a great idea. An audio letter. When it proved to be the only one Jake made, she was disappointed. Blake never made it known how he felt, until he started to play it after both his parents were gone. They'd sit, drink some wine, or smoke a joint, in the early days, and listen to them talk to Blake. She thought it was the coolest thing. And as the years passed, she thought it was the most precious thing. She didn't have any recordings of her parents, and their voices existed only in her memories, which became faded and frayed over the years.

He wrote a novel about his mother's early onset Alzheimer's that was published by a small independent house and that got him promoted. He hated the publish-or-perish game, but played it anyway, because he loved teaching. He loved reading his kids' writing. He chased the tenure demon until finally he got that prize. She was proud of him but he didn't really care. As long as he could write when he wanted to and get paid for something that he loved.

She was always his first reader of whatever he came up with, whether it was poetry or fiction. Her opinion mattered more than any editor, or colleague, or other writer friends he had.

She always wondered if he'd ever solve the crystal mystery. One day she noticed a small ancient photograph next to his typewriter, a man she'd never seen before. She asked him about it.

"My grandmother's brother," he said. "He died in 1918."

He said that he wanted to learn about that guy too, but there was even less about him than the family crystal. But he felt that the two threads were related.

"It's something to do with my family," he said. "Something to do with how they came here, maybe why, I don't know. How they finally belonged?"

She wanted to draw him out a bit, but wasn't sure how.

"Do you finally belong?" she said.

"I know I belong to you," he said.

"This I know," she said. "I mean, was there a time when you felt you didn't belong?"

"To what?"

"To your family. To your life."

She was getting deep, his Molly. When she went deep, he always followed. It didn't happen often, but he believed that she knew way more about life than he did. Her intuitive self was wise in a way he wished he could be.

She could tell he was thinking back, back, back through his life to give her an answer that would satisfy her.

"There was one time," he said. "I don't know if this is what you mean. We were kids, Jake and me. I helped him in a way that protected him, I think."

"You mean you came to his rescue?"

He laughed.

"I don't know if I'd go that far, but I think he may have felt something like that. It changed us, our relationship as brothers."

In the Sahara

Blake's parents would kill him if they knew he was here, especially with Jake. But he had no choice. Saturday was the only day Romano would agree to. If he didn't show, they'd never be able to work out an arrangement to keep kids from getting beat up. Romano specifically said Sunday wouldn't be acceptable because he had to attend church with his grandmother. So Blake gave up his Saturday at synagogue doing the junior congregation that he hated anyway. Jake never went, because he didn't attend Hebrew school yet.

Blake started out of the house as if he was going to services, wearing his good clothes. He made sure his mother saw him and said goodbye. Jake was waiting around the corner; he'd told their mother he was going out to play, and she had no cause for concern, or questions. But Blake had never lied like this before. He met Jake, out of sight of their mother's eyes. They didn't talk. The only sound was

Jake snapping his gum every few seconds. Jake wore his torn dungarees and ripped sneakers, Blake his pressed pants and white shirt.

When they were a full block away, Blake finally unbuttoned his shirt. It was going to be hot. But the Sahara would be cool.

Rounding the corner of Utica Avenue, the small gray building down the block seemed more than abandoned; it seemed forgotten. Particle boards had replaced the windows, the sidewalk in front of the entrance was cracked and uneven, weeds grew around the canopy's supports. Part of the maroon fabric had been ripped away, so only "ahara Cocktail Lou" was still visible. There were official notices stapled to the front door, now cheap wood instead of glass, warning trespassers to keep away, by order of the New York Police Department.

Surrounded by the heating asphalt of an empty parking lot, and in the absence of any trees, the Sahara shimmered in the morning sun.

Blake noticed a few long jagged cracks in the building's concrete. This place had been empty a long time, becoming almost invisible in the neighborhood.

Jake reached into his pocket and pulled out a stick of gum, handed it to Blake, who silently unwrapped it, stuck it in his mouth, then wadded up the silver paper and threw it on the ground. They walked along the driveway towards the rear. Blake glanced quickly around to see if anyone noticed them, but the street was deserted. This part of Utica was occupied only by small businesses, all of which were closed today, even Jack LaLanne's gym.

"Listen," Blake said, "I don't want you talking, especially to Romano. You're here because I need you here, to make a point to that asshole. You got it?"

Jake nodded. He'd heard about the Sahara, but never gone inside.

Once out of sight of the street, Blake visibly relaxed, but Jake was scared. Blake took his pocketknife, opened the blade, knelt by the basement window, feeling for the weak corner of the board. He shimmied the blade into the corner, slowly working it along until he could get a grip. When he had a solid handful, he eased the wood away from the frame. Jake helped Blake carefully remove the board. A whoosh of cool air hit them. They couldn't see inside.

After looking around one more time, Blake dropped into the darkness. The window was not high from the floor, so when he landed, his head was even with the ground outside. Jake joined him. They reached out, carefully lifting the board, replacing it in the opening. The board had a primitive strap tacked onto it. They used this to gently pull it back to its original place.

Standing in pitch black, the air was musty but cool. Blake couldn't see a thing, but knew his way around. His gum chewing sounded loud.

"Are they here already?" Jake said, his voice small.

"They should be."

Every time Blake came here he thought of what the Sahara must have been like when it was open. A rowdy nightclub, a place for mobsters to come and talk crime. He pictured black limos pulling to the curb, opened by a short fat guy in a uniform who needed a shave; long-legged beauties with teased red hair and too much make-up getting out in spike heels, on the arms of men twice their age chewing cigars. There would be a trio on stage, playing jazz in the smoky room upstairs. Maybe black guys, one on piano, a bass and drums. The room would be so loud that the music would be drowned out most of the evening. Now and then a table would burst into laughter. Clinking glasses ringing like bells, dozens of tiny orange lights dancing in the dark, the tips of cigarettes.

Blake knew that this room, the basement, was where the staff hung out, or where they came for more booze and other supplies. He pictured guys playing cards, cigarettes dangling from their lips, muffled noises above the ceiling. He used to think that maybe he'd get his first job here, busing tables. Although his mother once said something that made him think it'd never happen.

"I don't want you near the Sahara," she'd said. "I wish that place would disappear. It's ruining a good Jewish neighborhood."

Her wish came true, sort of. He was awake that night; it was late. He heard some of it, but saw nothing. He remembers the sirens, his father looking out the window on that hot night, trying to see two blocks down the street and around Utica.

"It's the damn Sahara," his father said to his mother.

The next morning was Sunday. He only wanted to get out of the house as fast as he could to go check out the scene.

"You stay away from that Sahara," his mother warned.

"Okay, Ma," he said.

That was one lie he knew would get him in trouble. He fetched his friend Heck, who lived next door, so they could go check out the devastation.

They practically ran there. He'd only ever passed the place walking his dog before school or on weekends. It was always closed, the parking lot empty, the doors locked, the inside dark and inaccessible. Turning the corner, it looked the same in the distance. Getting closer, Blake noticed all the glass, like diamonds sparkling in the street. Glass everywhere, tiny shards and larger pieces of windows. There was police tape across the front door, which still had one huge section of pane intact.

Then Blake saw the blood. There wasn't a lot, but he knew that's what it was. Some on the sidewalk, some in the street. It looked almost black. Some of it was dried, but there was one spot where it looked wet. Sort of shiny, like oil. Blake couldn't stop staring at the blood.

What happened here? Right around the corner from where he lived?

Heck had his head stuck through the front door, trying to see inside.

"It's a mess," Heck said.

"Watch it," he said, "You'll cut your head off."

Blake doesn't remember who finally got in there first. It was after all the glass had been removed, replaced with wood. It was on another Sunday when Heck came to get him, months later. Heck showed him the basement window with the strap tacked to its back. They dropped in, gently put the wood into the frame, and stood there in the dark.

Heck flicked his lighter. The small flame allowed them to see their way around. They didn't speak that first time, slowly finding their way to the main floor. The huge room that was the night club looked like it had been open for business the night before. There were still tablecloths on the tables, ashtrays full of butts, glasses everywhere, a few beer bottles, too. Blake could barely make out the wallpaper: camels and gently sloping sand dunes. So this was the Sahara.

Heck picked up a shot glass from one table and threw it across the room. It exploded like a gunshot. Blake threw a beer bottle. They spent a few minutes chucking ashtrays, bottles, wine glasses. Suddenly Heck held up his hand.

"Shh."

They held their breaths. Outside, a car. It sounded like it stopped right in front of the Sahara. Blake saw the front door through the room's entrance, now dark wood instead of clear glass. Someone was walking around out there. He could hear two voices. Men. They talked a bit, but Blake couldn't make out any words. Then the car started up and drove away.

"That was close," Heck said.

"Who was that?" Blake said.

"I don't know, but I don't want to find out."

It was easier the next time, and eventually they believed no one would be back. No repairs were ever made, the place was never razed. His mother said to his father that she heard the Sahara would never reopen. It became the first abandoned building in the neighborhood, and the secret clubhouse for different groups of neighborhood kids, all of whom allowed the others to use it when necessary. Blake knew that teenagers went there at night to drink and have sex. He'd seen used rubbers more than once, lying around like banana peels. And there were always fresh empties to smash against the wall. He and Heck and a few of their friends came there sometimes on the weekends to sit around and enjoy the place. And Romano, the Italian kid that Heck knew from around the block, often came here with his friends. Heck sometimes came with them too. In some ways Heck was more Italian than Jewish, but that was okay, because it would make today's meeting easier. He'd already be there with Romano, waiting for Blake and his kid brother.

Blake knew his way around now, even in the pitch black, and didn't need a lighter to find the stairs. They walked up slowly, listening. Blake thought he'd hear someone, but it was quiet up there. Reaching the main room, Blake saw the candle on a table, giving the only light. Romano sat, smoking a cigarette. He was Blake's age, twelve, but he always acted older, trying hard to be a tough guy. Romano had a few of his boys with him. Blake knew Ricky and Tommy, but there were two others he didn't know. Heck was there, too. Blake wished there were more of his friends.

Romano blew smoke into the candle flame.

"Blake," he said, almost laughing, like it wasn't a name but some dumb joke. "How you doin'?"

"I'm good," Blake said.

"And how's the kid?" he said, looking at Jake. Jake looked at the floor.

"He's good, too," Blake said.

He sat across from Romano and took a cigarette from the Italian. Jake had never seen Blake smoke before. He lit the cigarette off the candle.

No one knew who started it. Blake came home from school one day, found Jake on the front stoop, crying, holding his nose. Blake asked what happened, Jake tried to talk but Blake saw the blood. Someone jumped him and beat him up, leaving him to run home with a bloody nose.

Blake knew it was one of Romano's boys. Although Heck was friends with both groups, Blake and Romano only saw each other on their block, or around the corner near Avenue D, where the Italian kids lived. Blake didn't want an explanation. He just wanted to know where, and who. He ran around the corner, looking for anyone. When he saw Ricky, he chased him down an alley and cornered him. Blake's heart never beat so fast. He started throwing punches so fast Ricky was crying and begging him to stop in seconds. Blake felt like one of the kids he always avoided.

That was how it started. One by one kids were chased, cornered, hit, had their bikes knocked down from under them, bags of groceries knocked from their hands as they walked from Max's Grocery or from the Met Food on Avenue D. Blake was sick of the smell of broken eggs on the sidewalk all over the neighborhood. A kid from Blake's block, then a kid from Romano's block. It didn't seem like a game, or even some kind of war. It was just stupid, back and forth, and it wasn't going to stop unless someone did something.

So Blake talked Heck into calling Romano and

having a meeting at the Sahara to talk it out. He said he'd bring Jake, since that's how this all started. He wanted Romano to apologize to Jake, to his face. Jake didn't want to go, but knew if Blake said he needed to be there, then he needed to be there.

And now they were all here, but no one said anything. Someone had to start. Blake was about to, but Romano beat him to it.

"Don't we look all dressed up today," he said. Blake's white shirt almost glowed in the candlelight.

"My mother had to believe I was going to shul," he said.

"Lying to your ma," Romano said. "You'll go to hell for that one."

He changed chairs and sat next to Heck, opposite Romano. Romano's hair shone in the dim light, shiny black from too much Brylcreem, his spit curl dangling on his forehead.

"Nobody's going to hell, right Romano?"

"Just all the Jews," Tommy said from the shadows.

Romano laughed.

"Yeah," he said.

"What the fuck is that supposed to mean?" Blake said. This wasn't going right.

"You killed our Lord, that's what it means," Tommy said.

"What kind of shit is that?" Blake said. He kept hoping Heck would say something, but Heck probably had no idea what this was even about, not understanding any of it.

"You know what kind," Romano said.

"I think you better tell me," Blake said. He was shaking now, was glad it was almost dark, so no one could see.

"Christ killers," he said. "That's what kind. That's what all the kikes are."

Blake glanced at Heck, who looked completely lost. Jake thought he would pee his pants. Blake didn't know how to respond to this particular brand of bullshit. There was a split second of silence, and Blake could feel it slowly filling with hatred. He was stuck, no idea what to say.

A sudden burst of sound caused everyone to jump: Heck grabbed what was probably the only unbroken bottle in the Sahara, and smashed it against the edge of the table. Glass flew everywhere. He held the neck like a club, shoving it into Romano's face. Blake could see flecks of glass on Romano's cheek. Romano looked whiter than Blake's shirt.

"You take that back," Heck said. He shook the broken bottle under Romano's eyes. "I said take it back!"

"Blake," Romano said, "you'd better call off your friend here."

"I said take it back," Heck said. He pushed the bottle into Romano's skin. Romano looked down at the jagged edge of the glass, and seemed to hold his breath.

"I, I," was all he said.

"Say it was a mistake, right Romano?" Heck said. "Say you didn't mean what you said, about us Jews."

"Yeah," Romano said, his voice sounding small and high, almost a whisper.

"Okay then," Heck said. "He takes it back."

Heck threw the bottleneck across the room, where it shattered.

Romano wiped his face with the back of his hand. He did it in such a way that although they all thought he was carefully wiping tiny shards of glass from his cheeks, Blake knew he was also wiping tears from his eyes.

"I wanna talk about my brother," Blake said.

The candle flame bobbed up and down, causing their shadows to flicker and sway on the walls. They all waited for someone to speak. Blake thought he could hear everyone's breathing, distinct and separate.

Blake glanced over at Jake, and thought he was going to cry any second. Don't do it, he thought, trying to send thought signals over to him. If you cry now you might as well pee in your pants too, and make us Jews all look like pricks.

Romano said, smiling now, "So what I wanna know is, what's the problem?"

"Ricky hit my brother, that's what," Blake said. "Bloody nose. What the fuck, you know?"

"I did not!" Ricky protested.

Blake ignored him.

"My brother didn't do nothing. He's a kid. So that's why I went after Ricky. We had to. Right, Romano?"

"Stupid," Romano said. "Ricky, why'd you hit Blake's brother? What he do to you?"

"I didn't, Romano," Ricky said. He sounded very young.

"Romano," Blake said. "This ain't right."

Romano got up and walked over to where Ricky sat,

standing over him. Ricky put his hands up to protect his face, even though Romano just stood there.

"Ricky," Romano said.

"No," Ricky said.

"Take your hand away. I ain't gonna hit you."

Ricky lowed his hands, looking up at Romano, fear splashed across his face.

"I didn't," Ricky said softly.

Romano looked over at Blake.

"What do you think? Huh?"

"He's lying," Blake said, "right to your face."

Romano turned back to Ricky, and started slapping his face so fast that at first he couldn't react. Romano kept smacking him, on the face, on the head once Ricky put his hands up again, then on his shoulders, and finally on his back after Ricky bent over, trying to hide himself on the chair. Romano didn't stop. He didn't throw a single punch, but kept slapping until Ricky finally fell off the chair, and lay on the floor in a ball, crying, begging Romano to quit.

Romano finally stopped, standing over him. He waited a second for Ricky to calm down, then kicked him in the stomach hard, knocking the wind out of him. Then he sat down and looked at Blake and Heck.

"Okay?" he said.

Ricky cried quietly, hugging himself, trying to get his breath.

"Yeah," Blake said. "But if anyone's gonna give my brother a bloody nose, it's only gonna be me. I'm the only one. Understand?"

"Next time you just come talk to me," Romano said.

"But there won't be a next time, right Romano?" Blake said.

"Yeah." He looked around at his boys. "Right?"

The other Italians grumbled their agreements.

"Okay then. You guys got here first, so we leave after you," Blake said.

"Fair," Romano said. "Come on boys, let's go."

Heck, Blake and Jake sat while Romano and the other boys got up and headed back to the basement. They heard them walking down the stairs, then taking the board off the window. They didn't say a thing until after they were sure the Italians were outside. Blake could hear them talking, their voices fading as they got further from the Sahara.

"Shit," Jake finally said.

"Yeah," Blake said. "Give us some gum, Jakey."

Jake took sticks of gum out of his pocket, gave one to Blake, one to Heck, peeled one himself and popped it in his mouth. They all chewed loudly.

"What about Ma?" Jake said. "We can't go home yet, right?"

"I'll tell her the services ended early today."

Heck took out his sunglasses, put them on, and then blew out the candle.

"Don't fall down the stairs, Jake." Heck said, mocking him.

"Shut up, Heckman," Jake said.

Blake smiled to himself in the dark as they descended to the basement. This beat junior congregation any day.

And Now

Blake is an old man? How did that happen? Seems as quick as turning a page in a book. And what did that make Molly? She surely didn't look old in Blake's eyes.

Their marriage, their moving from one small Colorado town to another until they found their little mountain paradise, the birth of their son, the huge fights where Blake sometimes thought they might not make it (one time he had a bag packed and was headed to the airport, for a ticket to anywhere), dozens of Christmases, and equal number of Chanukahs which meant almost 2,000 candles lit through decades, and now a grandchild? He's some kind of grandfather? And again, what did that make Molly? His Molly? A grandmother?

Well, to be fair, she's Nonni. Or Nonny. He never asked her how she spells it.

Blake never thought about looking back, unless looking back would somehow work its way into whatever he was writing. But he knew it wasn't really his past. It was a past he could steal from, and as soon as the theft was complete and what was stolen morphed into his sentences, it was something else. He understood this from years of crafting memories into fiction, deeply felt emotions into poetry.

Molly didn't always understand this, the way she at first thought his family was screaming at one another in anger, as opposed to having a blast at his father's birthday party.

"That didn't happen like that," she'd say, reading a story.

"No, it's not what happened," he'd say, "I took what happened and had to shape it into what you're reading."

"Well, you still got it wrong," she'd say.

Like the story of the family crystal. She knew about it, because they had a few pieces prominently displayed in their home. She really thought Blake would dig up the truth about this beautiful glass. And when she read what he'd written, she was confused.

"So you never really found out much about all this stuff," she said.

"Mol," he said, "that wasn't the point."

"But I wanted it to be," she said.

"My sweet Molly," he said – and she loved when he called her that, "the point, I think, is the people I found."

"I like Aunt Rose," she said.

"I'm so glad you got to know her," he said.

Of course he meant the real Aunt Rose, his great-aunt his character was based on.

But he knew she wanted more. That was okay with him. That was Molly.

He still had a few pages of notes for this book he was finishing, but knew, now, that he wouldn't use them. There was no room for the kind of story he thought he might write, back in the beginning. Maybe those notes pointed to something more commercial? That was never his intent. He wanted to somehow write the truth, even if it was couched in fiction. Wasn't the best fiction the best stand-in for truths that were the hardest to write? In a nutshell, that was the summation of his whole career.

It was why his fiction would bring people to tears, over the decades.

"I can't believe you were able to write that, it must have been so hard," he'd heard more than a few of his readers say.

"Well," he'd think, but never said out loud, "that never happened."

He wrote a very long poem once, his tortured response to 9/11, as a former New Yorker. But it was about a tree that was in front of his childhood home. In the poem, he brings his son to see the tree of his youth, but when they get there, it's been cut down, and there's only a stump. He'd gotten it published and read it at a few readings over the years. And people would come up to him and say, "That's amazing that you brought your son to see that tree. How horrible that it's gone."

He'd thank them, and think, for all I know it's still there. This is fiction, in poetry. But I guess it worked on you!

And his sweet Molly still wanted the secrets of the crystal to be found out. But he would have to invent those secrets, which meant they weren't the secrets she wanted at all.

Not really. Even she'd know she was being fooled.

But when is a book done? When is the writing finished? He had a lot of very old books in his library, and in many of these, on the last page, after the last sentence, centered, on a line of its own, was "The End." He figured that 'in the old days' that's how an author let the reader know there was nothing else. Thanks for reading! Thanks for stopping by! Bye now!

And now he understands that the writing he's been doing today was, in truth, a way for him to avoid the calendar. Today was his father's yahrzeit, and so he had to light the candle for him. Molly had already gotten it out, and it sat on the stove, waiting for him. She'd even put a lighter there.

And lighting that candle also meant pulling out the recording of his parents. This was the first time his small grandchild was old enough to be curious about the candle. He turned on the stereo, went into his iTunes library, found the recording, and got ready to hear the words of his parents from so long ago.

He picked up the lighter. His grandson watched him, obviously curious. Rather than ask him, he went over to his Nonny, as he flicked the lighter, lit the candle.

"Nonny," the child said, "is it my birthday?"

"Not a birthday," Molly said. "Ask Poppa."

"Poppa," the boy said, watching Blake hold the

lighter to the wick. "Is it your birthday?"

"No," he said. "this is not a birthday candle."

"Can I blow it out?"

Blake laughed.

"No, we let this one burn. It'll burn all night, and tomorrow it will go out."

"Why?"

The age-old question.

"It's for my dad," Blake said.

"Who's your dad?"

"Here, come with me," he said, but the child stared at the flame, mesmerized.

"Go see," Molly said, as she wiped down a counter.

The boy came and sat next to Blake, as he checked the volume, then hit play.

The first voice was Jake's.

"That's Uncle Jake!" the boy said.

"That's right. He was young then."

"Were you young then?"

Blake laughed.

"I sure was."

"Who's he talking to?"

"He's talking to me, and Nonny."

Molly came in and sat with them. She always loved hearing Blake's parents.

And then his father's voice came through the speakers.

"Hey fella," Blake's dad said. "How you doing? Yeah."

Blake laughed, the way Jake did on the recording.

His father, struggling to behave as if he was in a true conversation with Blake. His father, so far away, so long gone.

"Just watched Denver beat the Jets!" his father said.

"What's the jets?"

"Shh," Molly said. "Let's listen."

The three of them sat on the couch, while Jake's audio letter played. Now for some reason, Blake couldn't tell if his parents did sound like he remembered, or if they didn't. He wasn't sure. He used to think that their voices were nothing like he remembered. But hearing their voices was comforting, even after all these years.

"That's your dad?" the child asked.

"That's him."

"And that's his candle?"

"Sure is."

"And that's your mommy talking, too?"

"Yes," Molly said, "that's Poppa's mommy, too."

"Everyone has a mommy," the boy said.

"That's right," Blake said. "And in a few months I'll light a candle for my mommy just like that candle burning is for my dad."

Blake could see the boy was listening hard. Trying to understand...what? He couldn't be sure.

And then, in just a few quick minutes, the recording ended.

"So?" Blake said, giving the child a loving grandfatherly pat on the head. "What did you think?"

They watched their grandson, then looked at each other. Molly gave Blake a quick wink, and a smile. He

246

knew nothing gave her more joy than sitting with this tiny bean, as he'd thought of him all through his daughter-in-law's pregnancy, and seeing him trying to make sense of his world.

"I like them," the child finally said, nodding his head, as he put a hand on each of Blake and Molly's knees.

"Yeah," Blake said, looking Molly in the eyes, "I like them, too."

The End

THANKS FOR READING!

THANKS FOR STOPPING BY!

BYE NOW!